Please feel frer
filters these c

Charlotte Michelle – charlotte_michelle@awesomeauthors.org

Sign up for my blog for updates and freebies!
charlotte-michelle.awesomeauthors.org

Copyright © 2018 by Charlotte Michelle

All Rights reserved under International and Pan-American Copyright Conventions. By payment of required fees you have been granted the non-exclusive, non-transferable right to access and read the text of this book. No part of this text may be reproduced, transmitted, downloaded, decompiled, reverse-engineered or stored in or introduced into any information storage and retrieval system, in any form or by any means, whether electronic or mechanical, now known, hereinafter invented, without express written permission of BLVNP Inc. For more information contact BLVNP Inc. The publisher does not have any control over and does not assume any responsibility for author or third-party websites or their content. This book is a work of fiction. The characters, incidents and dialogue are drawn from the author's imagination and are not to be construed as real. While reference might be made to actual historical events or existing locations, the names, characters, places and incidents are either products of the author's imagination or are used fictitiously, and any resemblance to actual persons living or dead, business establishments, events or locales is entirely coincidental.

About the Publisher

BLVNP Incorporated, A Nevada Corporation, 340 S. Lemon #6200, Walnut CA 91789, info@blvnp.com / legal@blvnp.com

DISCLAIMER

This book is a work of FICTION. It is fiction and not to be confused with reality. Neither the author nor the publisher or its associates assume any responsibility for any loss, injury, death or legal consequences resulting from acting on the contents in this book. The author's opinions are not to be construed as the opinions of the publisher. The material in this book is for entertainment purposes ONLY. Cover image from Shutterstock com.

The Mute Alpha

By: Charlotte Michelle

ISBN: 978-1-64434-010-3
©Charlotte Michelle 2018

Table of Contents

Prologue 1
One 6
Two 16
Three 26
Four 36
Five 44
Six 54
Seven 64
Eight 71
Nine 80
Ten 88
Eleven 95
Twelve 103
Thirteen 109
Fourteen 116
Fifteen 124
Sixteen 131
Seventeen 141
Eighteen 148
Nineteen 157
Twenty 164
Twenty-One 172
Twenty Two 184
Epilogue 191

To all my fans from Wattpad! Thank you for helping inspire me!

FREE DOWNLOAD

Get these freebies and MORE when you sign up for the author's mailing list!

charlotte-michelle.awesomeauthors.org

Prologue

Lucas

January 3, 2028

    Screams tear through the house, penetrating my ears as I try desperately to run against the crowd of people. I am pushed and shoved as my pack members flee the scene. I know what is happening. How can they just run away? How can they just allow their alpha and his heirs to simply die?

    The Cipher pack is difficult to explain. We have an alpha, but we also have elders. The alpha's word is law. He enforces the rules, and no one talks back or thinks twice about what he says. The elders are our most precious members, the older, wise people that the alpha seeks guidance from. However, if the role of alpha is compromised, the elders take control of the pack until a suitable alpha presents itself.

That is why the pack is fleeing. The elders, who are now in charge, have demanded them to do so. That only meant one thing, and I am not able to grasp the fact that my family is dead.

I sprint through the pack house, running through the empty halls until I get to the grand ballroom. I see my mother and brother lying dead on the ground, blood pooling around them. My father is struggling against a hooded man.

I watch as the hooded figure lifts up his hand, his fingernails elongating into sharp claws as he slashes my father's throat.

"No!" I scream, running as fast as I can to save the only family I have left.

My father's dark green eyes flicker to me, sadness consuming them as he shakes his head. He wants me to retreat, to run the other way.

I tackle the man in the hood to the ground, looking over my shoulder to tell my dad to run. But he is already lying on the ground, blood pouring out of his mouth as he stares lifelessly at me. How is that possible?

My eyes lower to see the gruesome wound on my father's chest. He is dead before I even got to the ballroom. I crawl over to him, dismissing the fact that my enemy is still with me. I don't care. I don't care if I die.

I lay my father's head on my lap, tears rolling down my cheeks as I hold him close in our last embrace. I am ready for the Moon Goddess to take me. I can't bear to live in this world without them.

I lean back and close my eyes, silently praying for the goddess to take my life as I sit here. May she be gracious and allow me to spend the rest of time with my family.

The man in the cloak walks towards me, his pace slow as he looms over me. I keep my eyes closed, but I still see the shadow of him lifting his hand and aiming for my throat. The last thought that enters my mind before I die is *mate*. I will never know who she is, and I regret the fact that I am forcing her to live a mateless life.

I feel the strong, piercing force of the cut across my throat. However, it is interrupted by a loud roar. I fall to my back, gurgling on blood as I struggle to breathe.

Figures run towards me, but I can't make them out. My vision becomes blurry as I am finally taken from this world.

* * *

A bright light shines on my eyes, causing me to squeeze my already shut eyes tighter. Why is a light being shown on me? Can't they see that I am sleeping?

I moan, raising my hand to shield my eyes as I roll onto my side. The movement causes discomfort on my neck, and I reach around to touch my throat. I feel thick, rough skin. I begin to panic as I sit up. My eyes open to a bright and clean white room. I'm in the pack infirmary. Why?

My father's beta, Grant, steps into my line of vision and looks at me with sorrow filled eyes. What happened?

"Do you remember anything, Luc?" he asks.

I try to recall all that happened, but my memory is foggy. I shake my head.

"Your parents and brother were killed. There was an attack. You were badly wounded," he says.

Thoughts swirl around my head. *They're dead? How can they be dead? How can I not remember them being dead?!*

How? I open my mouth and move my tongue to form the word. However, no sound reaches my ears.

As I look at Grant, I see that he didn't hear me either. I try again and again. But not a single sound is heard.

Grant's eyes become even sadder. "You lost your voice during the fight. The cut to the throat was meant to kill you. We stopped him in time to save your life, but there was serious damage done to your vocal cords. You are permanently mute."

Tears roll down my cheeks as I hear what he said. How can this be? Why couldn't he just kill me? Why did the Moon Goddess choose to punish me so?

"One more thing. With everything that has happened, you are now the appointed alpha of the Cipher pack," Grant continues to speak, telling me about all of the events that will need to unfold within the next few days to ensure pack stability.

I don't listen to what he says. This is too much.

To lose your family and your voice and to be given a huge responsibility that I was never prepared for all in one day is traumatizing. I'm only fourteen. I'm not ready for this.

I close my eyes as I cry. I should have just died.

One

Mae

September 13, 2036

"How does it feel to be eighteen?" my mom asks as I walk into the dinette.

Yesterday was my eighteenth birthday, and I honestly don't feel any different. I offer her a smile as I sit next to her and across from Uncle Trent. He gives me a wink before he continues a private conversation with Aunt Natalie.

Everyone has changed, mostly for the better, and my parents are closer than they ever were.

My mother has flourished with beauty, and her guilt for the death of my two siblings has slowly faded. Or at least, she's been able to cope with it. I never judge my mom for what she did. I wasn't born then, and it had nothing to do with me.

My dad is a wonderful father, and he is hardly ever blind anymore; however, keeping his wolf near the surface so that he can see tires him out quite a bit.

Trent is back to normal as my mother says. Apparently, he closed himself off from her, but I never had a chance to witness it. He's a great uncle, and he loves Natalie despite the age difference. They have a young boy, Michael, who looks just like his father with the smile that reaches his eyes.

Jesse and Mason. If I don't have my parent's love to envy, I will certainly be jealous of Mason and Jesse's. They look at each other as if they are the last thing they will ever see. Mason always has an arm around her or is playing with her hair.

Jesse is also a mother of a young boy, Joey. He looks just like his mama with piercing eyes and dark hair. My mom says it's a shame we don't have another blondie in the family.

Yes, she still calls Mason *blondie*.

Jenny, Tyler, and their son, Duke, come over every Friday night for a cookout. Duke is sixteen—two years younger than me. He has grown into a good-looking man. He has his father's tan skin and dark hair and his mother's brilliant green eyes.

Everyone is happy, especially me.

Granted, I don't have a mate. But right now, I don't need one. I look at my family, and I am content. I can't ask for a better bunch.

At that moment, my father walks in from the backyard, walking over to give me a kiss on the top of my head. Then he goes and kisses my mother's lips. I watch in amazement as my father's eyes glow a bright cobalt blue. They scream power.

He has overcome so much.

Landon Grey Matthews is my role model. I strive to have the courage and the passion that consumes him every day. I hope one day I will be able to run the Shadow pack as he has. He took a crumbled pack at the age of sixteen and revived it. He now has over two hundred members, all loyal to him.

"Morning, everyone." He's sweaty. He must have gone for a run.

"Morning!" we say in unison.

My mother leans over and whispers, "Morning, baby," and pecks him on the cheek.

Yes, I am definitely envious of their love. After everything they've been through together, nothing can break them apart.

"Sorry I was late. I was meeting with an alpha," my father says.

That catches everyone's attention. We all put down our forks and look at my father.

Who would be contacting him? The packs have all lived in peace since Castor's execution.

"Who?" Mason asks, his spine straightening as he keeps his full attention on what my father has to say. He has his arm over the back of Jesse's chair.

"A pack from the Wyoming territory. The Cipher pack."

I arch an eyebrow. I've heard of this pack. That was where the Rogue Massacre took place. Many rogues stormed through the pack and murdered the alpha family, all except the youngest son, Lucas Donovan.

He was given the pack at the age of fourteen. Since then, the Cipher pack is in turmoil. Half barely follow Lucas's demands, and he struggles to keep the pack united. It's even harder when he can't speak to them.

I hear he uses his mind link, but when speaking to such a large audience, it is hard to link to everyone, and most of the words get lost along the way. Poor kid.

I was ten when the massacre occurred. It was a long time ago, but the pack is still in pieces.

"What did Lucas want?" I ask.

My father looks at me, a smirk playing on his lips. He's pleased that I am paying attention.

He's been having me sit in his alpha-beta-gamma meetings so I can learn what it is to be an alpha. When he calls Mason and Trent to his office and speaks to them about the events that go on throughout the packs, I stay with them as they discuss.

"He's searching for his mate."

A frown plays on my lips. He still hasn't found his mate? He has to be twenty-two now. He should have found her four years ago.

I can't help but feel sorrow for him. He has already lost a lot and on top of that, his voice. Perhaps when he finds his mate, he will learn to beat his condition. Just like my dad did.

"He will be meeting with the pack tomorrow to see if she is here. If not, he will move on to the Rose pack."

Everyone nods and goes back to eating their breakfast.

I wonder what he looks like. I also wonder why he lost his voice. Stories are told that half of his throat is missing. Some also say that he simply just chooses not to speak out of respect for his fallen family. That's what I hate about stories passed through one another—they are hardly true.

I dismiss myself from the table and give my mom a hug before I head outside, feeling my wolf itching to come out. I call upon her, closing my eyes as I embrace the change. My skin tingles, and my stomach drops as I fall onto all fours, a hairy beast.

Just as I look similar to my father in human form, I also share the white wolf that he has.

I was born with golden hair; however, as time passed, it slowly transitioned to a milky brown. My eyes are hazel, which I think matches the brown better.

My wolf claws at the ground, and I grant her what she wants: to run. It gives me such a high to run until I no longer can. It means I have pushed myself. And every day, I go just a little bit further.

Having a big pack and an alliance with our neighboring packs gives us a lot of lands to cover. We seldom worry about running too far because it will take nearly a day to reach the borders of our territories. So I run until my heart is nearly out of my chest from exhaustion and my legs collapse underneath me. Even though that sounds painful, I love it.

I lie on the cool forest ground after running for five hours. To a wolf, that is a perfect run. I know in human form, I'd be dead on the pavement if I ran for five straight hours. It is amazing how much endurance a wolf truly has.

Birds chirp from the trees above me, and I lift my head, shifting my body, so I am lying on my hip and elbows as I pant, listening to the songs they sing. My breathing is heavy, but as I focus on the music of nature around me, I slowly begin to regain my energy.

The sunlight beams through the leaves of the trees, and I crawl away to find shade. There is no way I am basking in the sun with all this fur on me. Just as I get used to the music, it stops, and harsh flapping of wings take its place. My ears perk, searching for what startled the birds. I get to my feet, my tongue lolling out as I pant. My eyes scan the area, but I come up short.

Maybe the birds decided to just move on. Perhaps I should too.

I begin to walk home, still too exhausted to even brisk walk. I start to feel a presence with me, and the hair on my nape stands up. Someone is following me. I twitch my ears, trying to catch a sound, a breath, a sniffle, a crunch of leaves, anything. But I come up short.

No, there is definitely someone behind me.

I spin around and bare my teeth, ready to attack until my body shuts down or, shall I say, comes to life. I am frozen, gazing up at the handsome man in front of me. I inhale deeply through my nose, breathing in the pine and smoke scent that strangely feels so familiar.

I don't need my wolf to tell me. I already know I am going to love this man forever. I don't know who he is or where he came from, but he is mine, just as I am his.

The man before me is wearing nothing but black low-waist track pants. His chest is bare, available for my admiring eyes. He has a large tattoo on his left pectoral, but I can't make it out as my eyes rise to meet his big brown doe-like ones that hold so much sorrow. His blond hair is mussed, falling across his forehead as he gazes down at me.

I notice a horrid scar on his neck but don't think twice about it as I contemplate on shifting back. I just met the man, and I don't have a change of clothes. I back up a few steps and look around.

Maybe I can cover myself up with leaves? Like how Tinkerbell does it?

Yeah, go make a leaf dress. I roll my eyes at my stupidity.

When I look back up to my mate, he's no longer standing in front of me. I look around, panic building inside of me. Why would he leave? I quickly follow his scent, catching up to him in no time. He's just walking away at a brisk pace.

I nudge his hand, yelping at the shock that starts at my nose and spreads through my body at the contact. My mate looks down at me as he takes his hand away. I mentally frown. Why is he rejecting me?

He can't possibly be…Can he? He hasn't even said a word to me, and he just walks away?

No, I will not let him get away from me.

I follow him as he continues to walk, determined to talk to him and ask him why he is dismissing me so quickly without even knowing who I am.

My mate takes us through the forest. After a couple of minutes, we come across a camp of tents. I look to see many people gathering food, starting fires, or even collecting firewood. Everyone seems to have a job and is doing it. I trot forward and gently nudge the first woman I see. When she sees me, she instantly understands what I am asking for.

Everyone in the werewolf species understands the difficulty of having to shift back nude. It is aggravating, and we do well to help each other out.

The white-haired, older woman comes back with a light blue sundress, and I take it in my mouth, running into the trees to shift back and throw the dress over me. It's a little big for me, but I am just grateful to have clothing.

I emerge from the tree line and scan for my mate. But of course, he doesn't wait for me.

Jerk.

I breathe in, following my instincts as I storm through the camp. I ignore the stares I receive. I know they are wondering who I am and what I am doing here. But this isn't their territory. They are camping out on the Prowler pack's land, and I have every right to be here…More so than they do.

I find my mate sitting in a lounge chair by a tent, looking at a fire, and this angers me. Why would he just dismiss me so easily?

I stomp towards him, but I come to a halt when I see a lone tear rolling down his left cheek. My heart squeezes tight as I watch him. Why is he sad?

His beautiful brown eyes look up at me, and I tilt my head to the side as he takes me in. Then, he shakes his head. He just sits there and shakes his head as another tear rolls down his cheek. I know what he's thinking. He wants to reject me.

Say it. Just say it.

"Can I help you?"

I spin around and take a step back as a man in his mid-forties stands in front of me. He has salt and pepper hair and an afternoon shadow that is sprouting on his face. His dark brown eyes glare at me, waiting for my answer.

"I…I—" I stumble over my words, but I am grabbed by the wrist and pulled back a few steps. I spin, ready to attack the assailant; however, I am met with a pitched tent. I feel my shoulders rub against a warm, bare back. I look over my shoulder to see my mate standing in front of the older man.

I peek over my mate's shoulder to see him glaring at the man; however, they don't speak. They must be using their mind link.

Salt and pepper man looks over at me, his eyes wide. "Forgive me, miss. I didn't know."

Didn't know I am the alpha's daughter or the mate of a pack member?

"I'm Grant, beta of the Cipher pack."

I nod. "I'm Mae Matthews, daughter of Landon Matthews," I say, almost as a warning and a sense of security washes over me.

No one in their right mind will harm the daughter of an alpha.

Grant looks over at my mate again, and I grow curious as to what they are saying. Why can't they just say it out loud?

Grant frowns as he meets my eyes again. "Lucas wants you to reject him."

My eyes widen as I process what he is saying, not only the fact that my mate wants me to sever my connection with him but what Grant just called him. Lucas...Lucas is the alpha of the Cipher pack. He is the poor boy who lost his family and his voice at the age of fourteen.

And now he wants to lose his mate.

I am sorry, but no way in hell is that happening.

Two

Mae

September 13, 2036

I stand before Lucas, staring at him with a blank expression as he tries desperately to avoid my gaze, but I do well to ensure he does not. He will look at me and see that the Moon Goddess does not make mistakes and that we are destined to be mates.

Rejecting each other will be a grave mistake.

"I will not." I declare.

Lucas's eyes flicker over to Grant. His expression is hard and angry.

"Lucas says that he does not want you."

"He came looking for his mate! Well, here I am!" I holler, lifting my arms up at my sides.

Lucas turns and walks towards me, placing a hand at the crook of my neck and pressing his thumb against my throat. I struggle to breathe, glaring at him for doing this, but deep inside, I know he is angry, hurt, and tormented.

"He claims it was a mistake to ever come to seek you. The Cipher pack doesn't need a luna," Grant says.

I look over at him, wishing that he didn't have to stand here and be the mediator for us. But the only way to speak to Lucas is to be marked by him, and at this rate, that won't be happening any time soon.

I blow out a frustrated sigh and push on Lucas's chest. "You will not touch me in such a cruel manner. I don't care if you regret finding me. I was taught at a young age to bless every day and everything you are given. My family is bathed and born from bloodshed, just as you were. I know what you went through, and I know that you are still haunted. But I will not reject you because I do not so easily throw away the blessings that are given to me."

I release a deep breath and watch Lucas, daring him to give me another comment of rejection. I swear I will attack him here and now if he does. The Moon Goddess doesn't make mistakes.

Lucas looks over at Grant and nods, telling him to leave. I stare after Grant.

Well, how are we supposed to communicate?

Oooh…He doesn't want to.

I look back to see Lucas sitting in his chair again, so I walk over and take a seat on the ground next to him, staring at the fire.

"Beautiful day, don't you think?" I say, a smile on my lips. "The weather lately has been so crappy. All this rain and the bloody heat is killing me. I'm excited about winter though. When the snow is on the ground, you can barely see my wolf. I blend right in." I turn, sitting on my knees as I look up at him. "No one can see me. I am lucid and sly. The deer don't stand a chance." I cross my arms. "I bet you have a handsome wolf. Dark gray? Black? Whichever it is, I am sure I will see it soon. Did you know that wolves only mate once? That if their mate dies, the wolf will detach from the pack and they will wander alone until they die. Sad, isn't it? That's also what happens when a werewolf is rejected. Is that what you want?"

Lucas's eyes meet mine.

I shrug. "Hey, don't worry. I can talk enough for the both of us."

And so I do. I ramble on about my favorite Disney movie, what music I like to listen to, and my most embarrassing secret. I notice his posture changed from rigid to relaxed. I even see him smile a few times as I babble.

His smile sparks accomplishment in the pit of my stomach. I can live off his smile. I will work every day to ensure that it remains on his face.

Lucas closes his eyes in the middle of my story about how I fell down the stairs and broke my arm. When I finish it, he lifts his head and leans over, so his face is only a few inches from mine. His doe eyes stare into my soul, searching.

I ache to reach up and trace his prominent cheekbones, his sharp jaw. His face is chiseled by a god himself.

Lucas nods and reaches over to tuck a piece of hair behind my ear. His touch sets my skin on fire. He reaches into his pocket and pulls out a slick iPhone. He hands it over, signaling for me to program my number.

A smile stretches across my face as I punch it in and then hand it back. Lucas types something and a moment later, hands it back. I frown, confused before I remember that my phone is back home, considering I'm not able to carry it when I shift. I snatch it up quickly, looking down at the screen.

You win.

My stomach does a flip. The best two words I have ever read.

I quickly type back.

You won't regret this.

Lucas reads the message and responds right away without batting an eye.

We head home in the morning. I shall pick you up on our way.

And just like that, everything inside of me breaks. My heart stops, and I feel as if my lungs are constricted.

Too pleased with finding my mate, I forgot exactly what it meant. I have to leave my home, my family. I stand and shake my head, my eyes wide.

Lucas watches me.

Sure you don't want to reject me?

I peek up to see a grim smirk on his face.

Jerk.

He's trying to get me to reject him. He's playing with my heart.

I let out a growl and toss his phone at his chest. "Good try." I turn on my heels and storm back to the forest where I shift to my wolf and sprint back home where I will have to say goodbye to my family.

* * *

Lucas

I watch after her, feeling my wolf clawing to get out and follow her. She is right. Rejecting each other will only kill us, but I'm no good for her.

Who wants a mate who can't speak and an alpha who is weak and detests his job?

She is a strong woman—someone who has been trained since she was a child to be an alpha. She is fit for the job; however, I am not. I am a disgrace.

Half of the Cipher pack wants me killed. I see it in their eyes. I don't understand why…What did I do to make them want to kill me? Is it because I can't speak? Do they find it disrespectful for a man with such a disability to be their alpha?

I let out a sigh and drop my head into my hands.

"She's pretty."

I know that voice. I look up to see my best friend, Travis, sit beside me in another lounge chair. I shake my head; however, a smile plays at my lips.

Yes, she is. She has beautiful brown hair that reaches her mid back and bright hazel eyes that pierce my very soul. Her face is gentle, yet its features are defined. Her jawline is angular but in a feminine way. As I said, she is strong.

I will only hurt her, I tell Travis.

"I don't think that is possible, Luc. You don't give yourself enough credit," Travis says.

I stare into the fire. It is finally getting dark.

"Besides, she lives with a blind alpha. Who is to say she can't handle and love a mute one?"

Travis's words give me a flutter of hope. Of course, he is right. Alpha Matthews was blinded at the age of sixteen. He found his mate, who despite everything, loved him and helped him regain his sight. And they had a beautiful daughter: Mae.

Her name is so delicate, so sweet. I only wish I could say it from my lips.

She will grow to hate me for taking her away from her family. She will grow frustrated—

"You're jumping to conclusions, Lucas. You need to give her a chance. I know you're scared to love and trust again, but she was given to you for a reason. Stop trying to deny to Moon Goddess's gift."

I grumble, looking over at the pack members who accompanied me in search for my mate. These are the wolves that are loyal, that trust me. They will follow me until death. The other half of my pack remains at the territory with a loyal elder. She will keep everyone in order while I am gone.

I shake my head. I wish Gavin were still alive. He was meant to be the alpha. He would have been a good one. All I am is a disappointment. I have tried these past eight years to grasp the role of alpha, but for some reason, my pack is still split.

No matter how much I try to mend the pack, it only seems to drive the wolves away. I am tempted to cut them off, to urge them to create their own pack, but Grant talked me out of it. Having them create their own pack will only give them the opportunity to attack us.

So as much as I want to banish them for disloyalty, I will not.

"She's a trained alpha…" Travis says.

Yes, yes she is. The more Travis speaks about her, the harder it becomes to push her away. Mae is a remarkable woman. I know that just from listening to her ramble on about the weather and her favorite Disney movie. I know by the fire in her eyes when she denies to reject me.

Perhaps she is the alpha the Cipher pack needs.

* * *

As morning dawns, everyone packs up camp, and I dispatch to the Shadow pack. Perhaps I should meet her family formally before I tear her away from them.

Travis follows on my tail, and I look over my shoulder to see him grinning like a maniac.

"How do you suppose you will talk to them?" he asks.

I frown. Of course, I didn't think that through. They are not linked to me. I won't be able to communicate with them.

It is times like these that I am grateful to have Travis as my best friend. He is always thinking two steps ahead, always rational. Perhaps he should be alpha. He would have been if I died like I was supposed to. He's Grant's son, and the alpha position would have been passed to the beta line.

Travis and I enter the Shadow pack's land, and I see many wolves training on the grounds, snapping and clawing at each other. Also, children are playing in the designated area, where they are safe from the training wolves.

A blond man, dressed in only basketball shorts, withdraws from a fight with a dark-haired man to look over at me.

"Alpha Lucas. I am Mason, beta of the Shadow pack. What can we do for you?"

I am here for Mae.

Travis relays my thoughts for me.

"Ah, yes. She is inside." Mason turns and walks into the house, motioning for us to follow.

Travis and I share a look before I nod and we step into the pack house. Once we enter, we went straight to the kitchen table where I see Mae sitting, speaking with a boy around her age, a bright smile on her face. I don't ignore the anger that surges through me at the sight of her with another male.

Mae's eyes widen at the sound of my growl, jumping from her seat to look at me.

"Lucas!" she exclaims, looking over at the boy again. "This is Duke, my cousin." Mae quickly introduces us.

I study Duke, arching an eyebrow. He's lucky he's her cousin.

"W-what are you doing here?" Mae stumbles over her words.

I am here to take you home.

Travis relays. My beautiful mate looks at Mason, the beta, her features similar to sorrow.

"I thought you said you didn't want me." Mae crosses her arms, and I smirk.

She's defiant and difficult.

I don't. But as you said, separation will kill us.

Travis shoots me a glare, but I just nod my head, telling him to speak.

Mae's lips dip into a frown as she runs a hand through her hair. "O-okay. I just n-need to pack." She turns and walks up the stairs, not sparing me a backward glance; however, I watch her until she is out of my sight.

I am sorry, my little mate. You deserve better.

"You hurt her, and I'll rip you limb from limb," Mason says beside me, so nonchalantly.

I am amused by his threat, but I know he will not hesitate to follow through with it.

If Mason is only the beta, I wonder how bad her father will be now that Mae is my mate.

Three

Mae

September 14, 2036

Tears roll down my cheeks as I shove essential clothing into a duffle bag. My ceiling fan blows at full power, cooling down the heat that is pricking at my skin as anger and frustration overwhelm me.

I was expecting Lucas to just head back to the Cipher pack without me. I didn't actually believe I had to say goodbye to my family so suddenly. But I shouldn't have been so unreasonable. Mates are not capable of leaving the other behind.

I'm just not ready to leave. I just met Lucas yesterday, and now I have to leave the only place I have ever known, the only people I have ever known.y

After putting together a collection of toiletries, shoes, my favorite outfits, and a few family pictures, I throw the bag over my shoulder and run down the stairs to see Lucas sitting at the kitchen table. He is carving his nail into the wood, his expression blank. When he hears my approaching footsteps, his eyes lift to meet mine.

I take in the man who is standing beside him. He is tall and thin with brown wavy hair and green eyes. He offers me a smile and then his hand.

"I'm Travis. Pleasure to meet you, Luna Mae."

My heart does a flip at his words. I am now his luna.

Lucas stands, walking over to grab my arm and pull me a step towards him. He looks into my eyes as Travis says, "He's sorry."

I don't take my eyes off my mate as Lucas's hand reaches up and brushes away my tears.

"He promises he will work every day to make you happy at your new home."

I nod as Lucas offers me a tiny smile.

Loud footsteps resound from the hallway, and I look over to see my father storm into the room, grabbing Lucas by the collar of the shirt and pressing him against the wall. "Listen here, pup. My daughter is a spectacular girl. You are lucky to have her as a mate. So if I hear that you hurt her or make her the least bit unhappy, I will come to Wyoming myself, and I will make sure you never have children. Got it?"

I bit my bottom lip at my father's threat. Uncle Mason has beaten him to the punch, but it's a father's job to defend their daughters.

I wrap my arms around my dad's waist, causing him to release Lucas and hold me tight, kissing the top of my head.

"This is all too soon, Mae."

I nod, gripping his t-shirt as if it is the only thing keeping me rooted. "I know. Where's Mom?" I ask, stepping away from him.

"She's outside with everyone else," he says.

I turn and exit the house, nearly running into my mom's waiting arms. Tears are streaming down her face as the clutches tightly to me.

"You need to be strong and remember everything we taught you." My mom steps back, holding my face in between her hands. "You are beautiful and wise and an alpha. You are important. Don't ever forget that." She offers me a smile, nodding slightly as she gives me a kiss on the cheek.

"I love you so much, Mom," I whisper.

I say my goodbyes to everyone; even Aunt Jenny and Uncle Tyler came to wish me well.

It is as if I am ripping my heart out as I climb into the large Chevy Silverado that one of Lucas's pack mates drove over. I sit in the back with Lucas, laying my head on the window as I watch until my family is out of sight.

I don't try to stop the tears that follow. There is no point. I know there will be many more to come.

We drive for a good hour until I finally look over at Lucas, taking in his posture and his sullen expression. He doesn't want this. He said so earlier today. He doesn't want me as a mate, and he doesn't want to be committed to me.

Will I ever be happy again?

It's so rare to find mates who are in a loveless relationship, but it's not unknown. I just pray that is not the case for us. I want nothing more than to fall completely in love with this man, but I need him to fall for me too. I will not let him break my heart and in the process, break me.

Lucas, feeling my gaze, turns to look at me. His eyes hold their own sorrow and pain. Because he doesn't want this future? Because he doesn't want to love again? Is he afraid that I will abandon him?

Lucas takes out his cell phone and begins typing. I can't help the butterflies that erupt in my belly as my phone dings. I check the screen.

Please don't cry, mo ghrá.

I look up at him, confused with the last two words. What language is that? Lucas frowns before he types again.

Forgive me. I am used to my pack understanding Gaelic. It means "my love."

I blush a deep red as I read his message. I turn to face him, tucking my leg underneath my butt.

"You're Irish?" I notice Travis in the passenger seat turn to look over his shoulder at me.

He has a smile as he nods. "We all are."

"Cipher is French," I say.

The original Cipher pack was mainly French. It was named the Cipher pack because when Irish settlers were first moving to the States, the pack kept Irish wolves hidden, a secret. That is the meaning of Cipher, is it not?

I feel my eyes widen at this newfound knowledge.

This is the most fascinating thing I have heard in a long time. I have never understood the names of the packs; however, the Cipher pack is a paradox in itself.

I cross my arms and let out a huff.

"Over time, the Cipher pack has become mainly Irish. If any member is not Irish, they simply learn the language," Travis tells me, now facing front.

I glance at Lucas.

"Why?"

Travis doesn't speak because Lucas is typing away on his phone. Upon the ding, I am already reading what he wrote.

It's a way to maintain pack secrets. We hardly speak our foreign tongue inside our territory, only when we're amongst strangers.

That makes perfect sense actually.

Hmph. Smart.

I smile as Lucas is actually opening up to me. I wouldn't have expected that so soon.

"Donovan?"

One of the first Irish surname listings.

I notice how proud he is of his name, of his father's name. I watch as something ticks in his eyes, and I know his train of thought is going down the same track as mine.

"It's a beautiful name. Lucas Donovan." I smirk. It flows smoothly.

My mom was French. She wanted a boy she could call Luc. So they named me Lucas.

I am pleased he is telling me so much about his family. It also gives me insight into his past and the man he really is.

Gavin is a thick Gaelic name.

I furrow my eyebrows. "I-I'm sorry...Who's Gavin?" I ask, looking up from my phone.

Lucas's lips settle into a deep frown, and I mentally curse myself for saddening him.

Stupid girl. I growl to myself.

"Gavin is Lucas's brother." Travis pipes up from the front.

I mentally slap myself. Of course, he is his brother. Anyone with a brain could have figured that out. He wouldn't just be talking about some random kid named Gavin. Besides, I'm pretty sure I read about Gavin's death when I was studying the Cipher pack many years ago. How could I have forgotten?

"I'm sorry," I whisper.

Lucas turns his body to face me, his face hard to read.

He types.

I will tell you everything you want to know about my family, mo cheann donn. But I want to know more about you, other than how much you love The Lion King.

I am going to have to install Google Translate on my phone if he keeps speaking to me in Gaelic...not that I mind or am turned off by it.

"*Moe Chiann done?*" I speak.

Lucas's face breaks into a large smile at my lame attempt at what he just typed. It's hard when I can't hear him say it.

My brown one.

He reaches over and touches my brown hair, and I blush profusely. He has such an effect on me. It doesn't help that he keeps using endearments when speaking to me.

"You sure you want me to babble on about my life?" I ask.

"No." Travis declares from the front seat.

I arch an eyebrow at him, silently urging him to fight me. I'll take him down.

Lucas nods, ignoring his friend. I take a deep breath, preparing for the long speech. I notice Travis cringe, causing me to sputter and laugh obnoxiously and unattractively. I double forward as I laugh, but I don't care.

I can go on for minutes at a time until I can no longer breathe.

When I stop, I see Lucas is still smiling widely at me, clearly amused. Travis is just shaking his head, looking back to make sure I'm still alive. I ignore them and start my life story.

"I was born on September 12, 2019. I have no siblings, which I am sorry for my dad. The Matthews line will end with me, and the Shadow pack will be passed to Joey, my cousin...I guess. I don't really have many friends, considering everyone is either much younger or much older than I am. But my cousin Duke was always close to me. Ever since I was a child, I dreamed of having the love my parents have. The whole disability-against-all-odds-evil-Castor-murderer-love-overcomes relationship was very appealing to me. It reminded me of a fairy tale.

"So, on my thirteenth birthday, I wished for my mate to be a man similar to my father. Someone who had a troubled past or even a disability. Don't ask why I find it extremely attractive." I peek up at Lucas to see him squinting at me, and I admire him more.

His perfectly tanned skin, his toned waist, strong arms, gentle face, and his beautiful doe eyes get me every time. I hardly look at the scars on his neck. Sure, I see them, but they don't bother me.

"Now, I find it totally sexy." I slap a hand over my mouth as I realize I just said that out loud to him.

Why do I not have a filter? I need one. And a little alarm to tell me to stop talking, to let others get a word in.

Yes, I definitely need one of those.

I gnaw on my bottom lip as Lucas's eyes spark with fire at my words. Down, tiger.

"What's he thinking?" I whisper over to Travis.

"Yeah…I don't feel comfortable saying it out loud…"

I am thinking that you're playing a dangerous game. You don't know what you're in for with me.

I clutch my phone tightly.

"I do though. I grew up with it. I lived it. I've seen my father struggle and my mom help. I know exactly what I am in for."

Your parents could speak to one another. You will never hear my voice, Mae.

I decide not to talk anymore, out of respect for Travis and the driver.

My father was never supposed to see again, but he did. Do not say never. *It is a filthy word covered in empty promises. I promise you, Lucas, that I will search every day to find a way to help you speak again if that is what you want. Just don't give up on me.*

Lucas reads my message over and over again. I see a sliver of hope flicker across his face. What I said was true. I do not believe that he is going to be a mute forever. How can I when I grew up with Landon Matthews? There has to be some sort of surgery or miracle that can give Lucas his voice back. Even if it has limitations, I am sure there is an answer out there.

Alright, mo cheann donn. I will not give up on you. As long as you promise to not give up on me.

I smile like a little idiot as I look Lucas in the eyes. I have to. He has to see that I am not lying when I give him my promise.

I hope my mother doesn't mind if I steal Mason's nickname.

"I promise, Blondie."

Four

Mae

September 14, 2036

I am not sure how Lucas liked that nickname, but I decided not to use it. He already claimed me as his Brown One, so I need to come up with something original.

The remainder of the car ride is spent with me babbling on and on about my life growing up. Lucas genuinely seems interested in what I am saying. I even see Travis tilt his head to hear me better. As I run out of fuel and material to talk about, I decide to ask Lucas some questions.

"How old are you?" I ask him.

I don't mind talking out loud. It doesn't bother me that Travis and Jake, the driver, can hear our conversation. I know they hear what Lucas is thinking anyway, so it is pointless to waste time typing it out.

My phone chimes.

I turned 22 last June 9.

So he's four years older than me. That's not too bad, I guess. It's actually kind of hot. I've always preferred the maturity of older men.

"What's your favorite movie?"

I'm sorry, but it's not The Lion King. I'll have to go with The Patriot or Shawshank Redemption.

I grin at the screen. It's hard not to smile whenever I get a message from him. Every chime signals how much closer we are at getting to know one another.

"Those are good movies. I approve."

The corners of Lucas's lips twitch.

"Hmmm. Most embarrassing moment?"

Lucas stares at me for a moment before his head dips down and he starts typing.

"Luc..." Travis gives a warning growl the same moment my phones chimes.

I look up at Travis, a little worried to read the message. But I muster up the courage and do so anyway.

Every time someone looks at me like I'm some dysfunctional kid. When they think, What's wrong with him? Why can't he talk? *and it's really bad when people speak to me as if they believe I will talk back.*

His response is a dagger to the heart. Not because he is aiming it at me, but because this is how he feels every time he meets someone new.

A frown tugs on my lips as I type back.

It does not matter what people say or think. If they look at you with confusion or disgust or whatever look they give you, I want you to give them an indifferent expression in return. Because screw them for thinking it is okay to treat someone that way. You're perfect, Lucas. You're exactly the way you are supposed to be.

Lucas just stares at his phone until he clicks it off and shoves it in his pocket. I feel my mouth gape open, hurt. He really has nothing to say to this?

Suddenly, Lucas reaches over and grabs my waist, yanking me until I am practically on his lap. He then opens the car door with one hand and kicks it open, keeping a tight grip on me as he jumps out of the car.

Oh. When did we get here?

I lie bridal style in his arms as members of the pack surround us. I was curious as to why he was holding me…They just want to say hel—

Oh hell no!

I let out a scream as someone yanks at my hair.

Let me at her!

I watch with wide eyes as his pack members scream profanities at him, trying to attack him. Travis and Jake act as a shield, keeping them off.

Why is this happening? I have never seen a pack who is so disrespectful to their alpha before. I glare at the uproar of disgraceful, disloyal members of the Cipher pack.

Lucas walks us to the house, pushing through the crowd. We are completely swarmed. This is complete and total chaos. How can this go on for so long?

"We wish it was Gavin who was alive!"

"I hope you die!"

"You never should have been alpha!"

I bury my face into Lucas's neck, their words wounding me. How can they say such things to him? I want to punish every single one of them for hurting him. No wonder he is so closed off and doesn't want to bring his mate into his world.

I hear a collection of growls, and I turn to see wolves running from the trees, attacking the crowd.

"Lucas!" I scream, and he holds me tight as Travis looks over his shoulder at me.

"It's alright, Mae. They're the wolves loyal to Lucas. They're just dispersing the crowd," Travis says.

I look back at the chaos, seeing that he is correct. They are snapping at their heels, steering them away from their alpha. I am glad we have more loyal wolves than disloyal. However, there shouldn't even be one wolf who doesn't devote its entire life to the pack. It should be cast out.

Once we reach the house, Jake locks the doors behind us and lets out a heavy sigh. I completely agree with him.

I'm exhausted.

Lucas gently sets me on my feet, keeping an arm around my waist as a precaution. The pack house is similar to my old home; however, it is a tad bigger. It has a rustic theme, holding antiques and a lot of wood fixtures. The mantle above the fireplace is oak. The chairs are chestnut, and the floor is dark wood or maybe cherry.

The kitchen is grand. Unlike mine, it's open. I am able to see the family and dining room by standing behind the kitchen bar. The counters are granite, and the cabinets are stained oak with silver handles. The appliances are all up to date. I can tell Lucas maintains his house.

"Who is this?"

My admiration of the house is cut short by a soft voice. I look over to see an old lady, around five feet, four inches tall with white hair and blue eyes. She gives me a delicate smile.

"Hello, I am Mae Matthews," I say, offering my hand to her, which she shakes. "I'm Lucas's mate." My spine tightens when her grip on my hand tightens a fraction, and her smile falters as anger flickers in her eyes.

However, she does well masking it. But my wolf is stirring within me, telling me to step away from her. She's bad news.

"My name is Elizabeth. I am an elder of the Cipher pack."

I let out a tight breathht breath. She's an Elder. Lucas trusts her enough to leave the pack in her hands. If he trusts her, then so shall I...until proven not to.

I know from experience and from many alpha lessons to never doubt your first instinct and impression, but I'm new here. I know no one. It's best not to make enemies on my first day. If I suspect anything of her, I will tell Lucas. But she's an old lady. Perhaps she was just displeased with the match.

"It's nice to meet you," I say, smiling back at her as politely as I can. I turn to see Lucas leaning against the kitchen counter, watching me with a pleased expression on his face. I quickly walk to his side, pressing my arm against his.

Being in contact with Lucas calms down my nerves.

Lucas drapes an arm around my shoulders and then tilts his head to the side, asking if I wanted to continue through the house. I nod. He grabs my hand and leads me away from Elizabeth.

"I hope to see you soon!" Elizabeth calls after us.

I tighten my hold on Lucas's hand, thankful he doesn't question me.

He gives me a tour of the house. If he needs to say something, he can just shoot me a text. But I pretty much figure out what every room is on my own.

The ballroom is my favorite. We don't have one at my old home.

It's extremely large, a Beauty and the Beast replica. It's so bright, and the floor glistens under the lights. The walls are adorned with windows that reach from floor to ceiling, allowing the natural light to enter. At the end of the ballroom is a small stage, probably for a band.

I notice how Lucas is uncomfortable standing here. He stares at the ground and shuffles on his feet, so I take him by the hand and lead him out of the room, which he seems grateful for. He takes us up the stairs and points out a gaming room where Travis and Jake are sitting on beanbags.

We continue until he stops in front of oak French doors. He types *"our room"* in his phone before he grabs the handles and pushes the doors open. I step in, feeling my jaw hit the floor. I feel as if we stepped into a palace bedroom.

The king-sized four-poster bed is grand with white nightstands on either side of it. At the foot of the bed, a little off to the right, there is a set of couches on a rug, surrounding a coffee table. They face the large windows that look out over the whole pack territory. On the wall opposite the bed is a mounted seventy-five-inch flat screen TV. On either side of the TV are doors. I am sure they lead to the en-suite and the closet.

I let out a breath and turn to look at Lucas. "It's beautiful."

He shrugs, staring into my eyes. I smile, reaching up to run my finger through his tousled hair. He is so gorgeous with the messy look.

I turn and run to the bed, plopping down on the plush mattress, letting out a content sigh. "Come." I pat the bed, watching as Lucas stares at me for a long while.

Is he contemplating coming to sit with me? It's not like I have cooties.

I am really sorry about earlier.

Lucas sends the message when he finally sits beside me. I roll and lie on my stomach, my head resting on his leg as I read his message.

"Don't be. I knew before I came that your pack has a rift."

Lucas slips his fingers through my hair.

"I will help you figure it out, Lucas." I promise, closing my eyes as I grow tired. It's been a long day, and this bed is too comfortable to not fall asleep on.

My phone chimes, and I lift it above my face.

You should get some sleep.

I nod and roll onto my side, pressing my face against his toned abs. Lucas sits frozen, not sure what to do.

"I will if you don't leave me." He sighs and continues to play with my hair as my eyes droop close again.

I feel so safe with him beside me. I honestly don't think I can fall asleep without him, too paranoid that someone would come and attack me. Not that I think Lucas would allow that to happen, but this is my first day here, and I haven't had the most friendly welcome.

As I drift off to sleep, I feel a pair of lips on my cheek, causing me to smile before my dream whisks me away from reality.

Five

Lucas

September 14, 2036

Mae falls asleep with her head on my left leg, and her face pressed into my stomach. I can't deny the fact that it feels so right to have her in my embrace, but I also can't forget where exactly I have taken her.

She is not safe with all these power hungry, disloyal mutts. I should have kicked them out of the pack a long time ago. Now they are a threat to Mae. I will not let anyone touch her. She may be strong and have the training I did not receive, but that does not mean I will not protect her, even against my own pack.

I run my fingers through her hair. It's so soft, just as her face is. She wears the most innocent expression when she's sleeping. When she's awake, she's nothing short of a firecracker.

I smile. I wouldn't change a thing about her. A pity, though, that she has to learn to cope with my disability. It's not fair that we have to communicate through our phones. I am sure it frustrates her. The only answer is to mark her, claim her as mine. And while I do wish to claim her, I don't want to tie her down to such a dysfunctional pack. Not yet.

I lean forward and place a kiss to her cheek, breathing in her vanilla scent.

Beidh mé tú a choinneáil slán, mo ghrá. (I will keep you safe, my love.), I mouth to her, silently hoping the words would reach her ears, but there is no way they could.

Slipping my arms under her knees and back, I carefully pick Mae up to reposition her, so her head is on the pillows. I cover her with the beige comforter and gently trace her cheeks with my fingertips.

She really is beautiful.

Before I get myself distracted, I turn and exit the bedroom, closing the door silently. I head to the game room and sit beside Jake. He looks over at me with his dark brown eyes, his eyebrows furrowed together. I lean back in the beanbag and watch as they play the newest version of Halo.

It is not safe for her here, I say to the both of them.

They don't take their eyes off the screen as their thumbs fly over the controllers.

Yes, it's not. You need to protect her, Travis says, and I want to thump him on the back of the head for his brilliant idea.

Thanks, stupid.

Travis smiles, effectively killing Jake with a headshot. Jake growls and drops the controller in mock anger.

I am going to call a meeting. Everyone is to be there. I will make it law; if you do not stand with the luna of this pack and me, then you will be exiled. I am sick of not being able to trust my pack.

I think that is very wise, Lucas. Is this something that Mae wants? Is she concerned? Jake asks, and I shake my head, leaning forward to rest my elbows on my knees and clasping my hands together.

She doesn't know I'm doing this. I will need you to stay outside her door during the meeting, Jake.

Travis looks over at me. "Shouldn't she be with you? The pack will need to meet her. It's hard to respect someone you can't see," Travis says.

Of course, Travis is right. The pack will not appreciate being ordered to respect Mae if they haven't met her. I'm sure it will only cause more uprising, but I need to make sure she is safe.

"She'll never leave our sight. Besides, there are more of us than there are of them—"

There is no 'us' and 'them.' They are still a part of this pack. I will treat them as such. If they so desperately want to stand against me, then I will more than gladly send them away. But while they are still here, they are our pack members. This feud has been going on for far too long.

Travis and Jake both nod. My father would not be proud of what I allowed to happen to his pack. He would be ashamed of me for letting it go on for so long.

We will have the meeting when she wakes, I tell them.

They instantaneously reach for their Xbox controllers and start a new game. I roll my eyes and leave the room, returning to where Mae is sleeping.

She hasn't moved from where I placed her. She is out cold. I smile and climb into bed beside her, remaining on top of the comforter. I don't want to make her uncomfortable in any way.

Just as my head hits the pillow beside hers, Mae's eyes open.

* * *

Mae

I feel the bed dip beside me, causing me to rouse from my slumber. Who would possibly be getting into bed with me?

I open my eyes to see Lucas resting his head on his pillow, gazing at me with his brown eyes. He offers a sweet smile before he reaches over and tucks a tangled lock of hair behind my ear. Lucas surprises me by making no move to leave the bed or to take his hand away. Instead, he cups my cheek gently, rubbing his thumb along my cheekbone.

"You're perfect," I whisper, copying his position as I place my hand on his warm, smooth cheek.

Lucas doesn't move a muscle. He just lets what I say sink in. Does he not believe me? Oh, if only he could see himself the way I do.

"How long was I asleep?" I ask, yawning. I remember Lucas can't speak, and I dig into my pocket to grab my phone.

Lucas smiles as he gives my cheek one more stroke before he takes out his phone as well.

Not long...Maybe thirty minutes. You can sleep more if you want.

I shake my head and move a little closer to him. His eyes widen slightly as our legs brush against each other.

"I'm no longer tired."

His eyes flicker down to my lips, watching as I take my bottom lip in between my teeth.

Yes, I may be teasing him, but he is driving me crazy with him so far away. I can see how hesitant he is, and I don't want him to be, not with me. He's not going to succeed in chasing me off because I'm not going to leave him.

You're playing a dangerous game, mo faolchu beag.

I stare at the screen for a long while before I peek up through my eyelashes to see Lucas grinning at me.

My little wolf.

He sends, and I blush red but return his smile.

"I am sure my wolf is nearly the same size as yours."

Lucas arches an eyebrow. I leaned over again, so our faces are a foot away. He lets out a low growl but grabs my waist and yanks me close to him, so we are pressed against each other. He grips the back of my shirt and leans forward to give my forehead a kiss. I close my eyes and sink into his arms, relishing in the contact.

"You're so warm," I whisper, wrapping my arm around his back and trailing my fingers up and down, feeling his muscles tense at my touch.

Lucas rests his forehead against mine, our noses nuzzling as his eyes focus on my lips.

Kiss me. Please, kiss me.

His lips merely brush mine when someone knocks on the door, causing Lucas to lean back but tighten his grip on me.

I imagine he instructed to let the visitor in through the mind link because the door opens and a tall blonde woman in her twenties walks in, wearing black shorts and a pink tank top.

She smiles, nodding. "Alpha, Luna."

Lucas sits up, inviting the girl in further.

"Travis just informed me that the pack has assembled."

I arch an eyebrow, sitting up as well to peek over at Lucas for some sort of answer. Why is the pack assembled? Is he having a meeting? Why didn't he tell me?

The blonde nods, turning to look over at me. "Hi, I'm Lisa, Travis's mate," she says with a sweet smile.

I return it.

"Hi. I'm Mae"—I jerk a thumb into Lucas's direction—"this guy's mate."

Lisa laughs, and Lucas smiles, leaning over to kiss my temple.

"Alright. Well, I'll see you down there." Lisa turns and leaves the room.

"What's happening?" I ask, rolling off the bed while Lucas heads to the closet and types on his phone.

There is a pack meeting.

My heart begins to race.

A meeting! I just got here, and I am already meeting the pack? The same animals that attacked us?

No, I can do this. It's not like they're going to hurt us during a meeting. They have to be somewhat civil.

"Should I change?" I ask Lucas, walking over to see him standing in the closet in nothing but unbuttoned jeans that hang low on his waist.

My mouth falls open at how incredibly good looking he is. I have never seen such a well-toned man. He doesn't look too buff with muscles that could pop or abs that are sharp enough to cut. Instead, his abs are evident, accenting the 'v' that starts at his hips and disappears low into the waistline. Veins can be seen on his arms, proof that he has a daily workout to maintain his perfect body.

Lucas looks over at me, smirking at my gawking.

I'm not even ashamed.

"You're definitely a gift to man…or women, rather," I whisper.

Lucas smiles, taking a button down shirt off a hanger and putting it on while walking over to me.

I instinctively help him button up his shirt, smiling up at him. "So should I change?"

Lucas looks down at me.

I'm dressed in faded bootleg jeans and a simple navy blue blouse that scrunches at my waist. The shoes I kicked off earlier are blue Tommy Hilfiger sandals. I think it's a pretty cute outfit if I do say so myself.

Lucas shakes his head and places a kiss to my forehead before he grabs my hand and leads us out of the room.

"Should I be nervous?" I ask, struggling to keep up with his long strides. "Because I'm nervous."

Lucas takes out his phone and texts with one hand, all the while never slowing down his pace.

I grab my iPhone from my back pocket the same moment it chimes.

I will never let anyone hurt you. So no, you don't have to be nervous, mo cheann donn.

My brown one. I am already familiar with that nickname.

I give his hand a squeeze and decide that I will just trust him.

We leave the pack house, and I am pleased to say it isn't total chaos. Instead, the whole pack is gathered around quite nicely, waiting for us. Travis and Jake stand in the front, facing the whole pack.

Lucas passes me off to Travis, giving him a hard glare as they communicate with one another. Travis grabs my arm, keeping me close to his side as Lucas stands before everyone.

"I'll translate," Travis whispers in my ear.

I notice Lucas's back grow rigid.

"He's saying, 'Recently, I found my mate, Mae Matthews. Upon her arrival here, she was attacked by a mob of Cipher pack members. I am standing here to tell you that that is not okay! She will be your luna. You will look up to her, and you will respect her as you should respect me. I know there are those of you who are loyal, and I thank you. However, as of now, if any of you show a sign of disloyalty to my pack or my mate, I will ensure you will be exiled or if need be, executed.'"

Lucas clenches his hands. He's outraged, and so his is pack. They begin screaming, throwing cans of soda or beer and fighting one another.

"Is this not clear?"

All of a sudden, as if a line is drawn between the pack, I watch as the people closest to us turn and face the other half of the pack. They're acting as a wall, protecting Lucas and me. I watch with horror as the men trying to get to us have nothing but hatred and anger in their eyes. They're crazed beyond the point of helping.

"Drive them away," Travis whispers.

At the order, all those loyal to Lucas shift to their wolves and stir the others away, biting at the flanks, even tackling some to the ground to show the threat is very serious.

Lucas turns and gives Travis a nod.

"He doesn't want you to see this." Travis pushes me into the arms of Lisa who tugs me away from my mate.

"N-no! Wait! Lucas, don't push me away!" I call as I watch my mate shift into his wolf, along with Jake and Travis. The three of them sprint into the chaos and join in on ridding the pack of the poison that filled it.

Six

Mae

September 15, 2036

It's almost one in the morning, and Lucas still hasn't returned. I tried texting him, but he didn't even reply. It wasn't until later that Lisa brought me Lucas's phone, saying that it was dropped when he shifted.

I curl up into a ball, hugging a pillow to my chest. There is no way I am able to fall asleep with everything that has happened. I don't understand why those people would choose to leave the safety a pack brings them. What did Lucas do to make them turn against him?

But then there are the wolves who would give their lives for Lucas...So what drew the line? What made some wolves disloyal and the others devoted?

I hear shuffling outside my door, and I know it's my guards switching shifts. Lisa ensured I had someone posted outside my room at all times. However, it barely settles my frantic mind.

What exactly is Lucas facing right now? Is he strong enough to not only defend himself but to carry out the punishment he enforced hours ago?

The bedroom door opens, and Lucas steps in wearing only basketball shorts. His hair is mussed, and there are scratches cover his chest; however, they're not deep. Lucas's eyes instantly meet mine, his breathing ragged as he heads toward the closet. Two seconds later, he is walking towards me with nothing but black boxer briefs.

My heart stops at his beauty.

Lucas pulls the covers back and slides in. I lie on my side, staring at him. He's exhausted, angered, and hurt. I can see all this in his eyes as he scrutinizes the ceiling as if it has the most fascinating pattern.

Tears gather, settling in his eyes until one escapes the edge. I move and wipe the tear away, resting my head on his chest. I don't understand his pain, but I've heard of it.

A pack is a family. We are all engraved into each other's hearts. We live off each other. And to have so many abandon him all at once, it's as if he's losing a big part of himself.

"It's going to be okay, Lucas," I whisper, lightly tracing the cuts on his chest with my fingertips.

Lucas wraps an arm around my shoulders, hugging me close to him. I feel him shake his head as he presses a kiss to the top of my head. I tilt back to look up at him.

"Let's talk about this in the morning. You need to rest." I try to give him a convincing smile, but it's hard when your mate is broken in front of you.

I wish I had the power to heal him, the way my mother healed my father.

Lucas just has to let me in. He has to claim me.

He nods, and I watch as he closes his eyes, keeping his arm around me. I snuggle close to him, hoping to comfort him as I close my eyes and drift off to sleep.

That was one hell of a first day.

* * *

When I wake up the next morning, Lucas is already out of bed, changing. I blink a few times until my eyes settle on his back. I watch as his muscles tighten as he lifts a dark blue t-shirt over his head. He then pulls on black basketball shorts.

Odd attire, I have to say.

Lucas looks over at me, his eyes shining for a moment. Then he nods, telling me to come over. I swing my legs off the bed, grabbing our cell phones off the nightstand. Lucas is confused when I hand him his cellphone.

"It fell out of your clothes when you shifted yesterday. Lisa picked it up for me," I tell him.

He nods before he begins typing.

Will you join me for a morning jog?

My eyes move to the top of the screen to see it is only six in the morning. I only got five hours of sleep last night. I'll fill that later on.

"Of course." I run to the closet and stare at my collection of clothes before I realize I didn't pack anything suitable for running. "What do I wear?"

Lucas joins me in the closet and grabs one of his t-shirts and hands it to me. I quickly switch my shirt and look down to see his shirt reaches just below my butt, not appropriate for running.

Lucas then hands me white basketball shorts. He really thinks I am going to fit in his basketball shorts? His waist is so much wider than mine. But alas, I pull the shorts on, and they instantly fall to my ankles.

Lucas laughs before he bends down to pick them up, pulling them to my waist. He then takes the strings and ties it tightly on my waist.

I give myself a few twirls before I am convinced that it is secured. Lucas reaches his hand out for me, which I happily grab hold of and let him lead me out of the bedroom. When we reach the kitchen, he releases my hand to grab two water bottles from the fridge. He hands one to me before he again grabs my hand and takes us outside.

Lucas takes us deep into the forest, and he knows exactly where to go. He must have been running all the time, and there's something undeniably hot about a man who runs.

Once we get to a trail, Lucas takes off in an even jog, glancing over his shoulder to see if I'm joining him. I smirk at him and run to catch up to him before I fall back into a smooth jog. The pace is good. It's enough to get our hearts pumping and to form a sweat but not enough to have us gasping for breath in five minutes. I could run like this for hours.

We are weaker in our human forms hence it's extremely healthy for us to keep up a routine workout in human form. While our wolves can sprint straight for hours, our human bodies break under all that pressure.

I uncap my bottle and take a swig of water, moaning softly as the water cools my scorching throat. Lucas looks over at me and stumbles a bit. I burst into a laugh, water spewing out of my mouth and nose. I double over, laughing and panting at the same time.

"I'm sorry. I don't know why I did that," I whisper, lifting my head up and brushing my hair out of my eyes.

Lucas just smiles at me, taking a drink of water himself. Lord, he's attractive when he's all sweaty…

Maybe he should take his shirt off…

I shake my head and then bump my shoulder with his. "Let's head back?" I ask.

He nods, and we begin jogging back to our house.

Whoa…Did I just say that? Our house?

Yes, you did. My mind taunts me.

I did.

It's our house now.

I smile to myself as I pick up my pace a little bit. "Race you back?" I don't even check to see if he agrees. I break out into a fast sprint, running as my legs cry in protest and my lungs feel as if they'll burst. But I just run, feeling him hot on my tail.

I see the tree line, and I smile. I'm going to beat him.

Lucas is behind me as we leave the forest and we race to the house across the large backyard. Once I am about ten yards away from the house, I feel an arm wrap around my waist. I scream as Lucas lifts me off the ground and places me behind him.

"Cheater!" I yell as he reaches the house.

I growl, running to pounce on his back. I wrap my arms around his neck and lean back, causing us to collapse on the ground. I act quickly and shimmy out from under him and straddle his waist. I cross my arms and glare down at Lucas who is just smiling up at me.

"You cheated," I mumble.

Lucas places his hands on my hips, giving them a tight squeeze before he sits up. My butt slides to his lap as he lifts a hand up to grab the back of my neck. His thumb brushes my cheek a few times as his eyes focus on my lips.

I hold my breath as he leans closer, our noses brushing against each other as his lips meet mine. My heart goes wild. I grip his hair at the back of the neck, holding him close as I kiss him back. Lucas nibbles on my bottom lip, causing my mouth to part so his tongue can slip in and dominate mine. I groan, causing Lucas to growl and tighten his grip on me. The kiss intensifies, causing me to curl my toes in my Nike's.

When he pulls back, he rests his forehead against mine.

"You can cheat whenever you want." I pant, and Lucas chuckles, giving my nose a kiss.

We sit like this for a few more minutes until my phone starts ringing. I jump to my feet and pull it out of Lucas's basketball shorts and see it's my dad.

"Hey, Daddy!" I say, a smile on my lips as I stare at Lucas while he grabs my free hand and intertwines our fingers.

"Hey, Mae. How are you doing?" my dad asks, his voice deep.

"I'm fine, just got back from a morning jog." I hope that explains why my breathing is ragged.

"So, I heard something peculiar happened yesterday at the Cipher pack."

My eyes meet Lucas's as he squints at the phone in my hands. I give his hand a squeeze, trying to calm him down.

"Oh yeah? What did you hear?" I ask.

"That Lucas exiled half of his pack because he wasn't able to control them."

I know what he is thinking. He is concerned about the man I am with, but it is a huge misunderstanding. This is what I hate about gossip. It's never true. There is always some sort of lie buried in there.

"He did exile half the pack, but he gave them a choice. They remained disloyal, so they had to leave," I explain.

Lucas has a frown on his face. How did my dad find out so fast? It hasn't even been twelve hours since it happened.

My dad is silent for a moment. "I'm proud of you, Mae. You're going to be a great luna."

I arch my right eyebrow. "Another test?" I mumble.

My dad laughs at the other end of the line. I love his laugh. It's so contagious.

My father used to always call me into his office or come into my room to talk to me about a very serious situation, either in our pack or in another. He will get to the point where I have to put in my opinion of the matter. He does this to see if my opinion is best for the pack or if I side with a greedy alpha.

"Oh, Dad. I think by now, you can trust that I know how to be a luna. I won't let you down."

"I know, sweetie. Hey, give my best to Lucas. I love you. Oh, and your mother says she loves you too." He hangs up, and I tuck my phone into the pocket of the basketball shorts.

"I need a shower," I say, turning to look over at Lucas.

He nods, grabbing my hand to lead me back into the house. We head upstairs to the bedroom where he locks the door, and I make my way to the bathroom.

I start the shower and grab a towel from under the sink, placing it on the toilet. Once the water is warm, I discard Lucas's clothes and slip in, feeling the water beat down on my sweaty body. I close my eyes and run my hands over my face.

Talking to my dad reminds me just how much I miss everyone. I am so used to waking up and spending the day with Uncle Trent or Uncle Mason training to fight. Or I spend the day with Aunt Jesse and Aunt Natalie to learn how to be a respectable luna, mate, and mother.

Sure, I spent a lot of time training and never really had time to be a kid, but I wouldn't give up my time with them for anything. Even though Mason and Jesse aren't related to me, they are just as much my family as Trent and Natalie. I feel like everything is complete at the Shadow pack and that I belong there.

I use Lucas's shampoo and body wash since I forgot to bring my own. However, I did bring my own razor.

After I rinse, I turn off the shower and hop out to grab my towel. I wrap it around my clean body and grab my brush. I comb my hair, gritting my teeth at the tangles. I also brush my teeth and apply a light coat of makeup.

I look around the bathroom for my clothes. Where did I put them? I growl when I realize I didn't grab any clothes!

I contemplate if I should just sprint to the closet in hopes that Lucas doesn't see me...Or maybe I could just tell him to leave?

I'm about to shout out to Lucas, but he knocks at the door. I jump back.

"Uh...I need clothes!" I yell, and I facepalm myself. *Just embarrass yourself more, Mae.*

Another knock at the door tells me he's there. I pull it open slightly so he can stick his hand in with a pile of clothes.

I grab them. "Thank you," I say, closing the door and pulling on the torn jeans and the orange spaghetti strap blouse he gave me.

After tossing my wet hair up into a bun, I pull the door open and step out to see Lucas standing with wet hair and fresh clothes on. He must have showered in the guest bathroom.

"So, what happened last night?" I ask, grabbing my phone from the pile of my running clothes as I toss them in the hamper.

We had to drive them off the territory. A few of the wolves got a little angry, and a fight broke out. It took quite a while to break it up, but there were no major injuries. Jake, Travis, and I stayed behind to ensure that no one tried to sneak back to the territory.

I frown. I hope this is all finally over. It is obvious that it adds a lot of stress on him; trying to run a pack who didn't want him.

"Well, I'm glad you made it back in one piece, and everything worked out." I walk over to him, placing a hand on his chest. "But let me get something straight. I am your partner now. I understand you wanted to keep me safe, but I will not just sit on the sidelines. I am meant to be by your side, and I don't want to be anywhere else. Okay?" I say, giving his chest a poke.

Lucas reaches up to cover my hand with his as he leans forward and gives me a quick kiss.

"Also, I want you to claim me."

Seven

Mae

September 16, 2036

Lucas stares at me with his lips parted and his eyes wide. He is completely taken by surprise. Hell, so am I. I never thought I'd be telling my mate to claim me as his, but here I am, standing in front of an amazingly attractive man, informing him that I want to be marked.

Werewolves usually mark their mates soon after finding them. I know Lucas is concerned about me leaving him, just like his family had. He's not ready to be so committed to someone.

But I fear not claiming each other soon will only result in us going crazy. Not knowing if he was going to come back to me last night tore me apart. When he marks me, I will be able to communicate to him through our mind link. We will no longer have to rely on our cell phones. And let us not forget how completely blissful it is to be connected with your mate in such a way. You feel as if you're invincible.

"Okay...So that was sudden, and I didn't mean to blurt that out."

Yes, you did, my mind tells me.

"But it's hard to be with you and not be completely with you."

Lucas just looks at me, his eyes trailing down to my neck and shoulder for a moment, indicating that he's thinking about it. I smile and step closer to him, slipping an arm around his neck. I use the hand at the back of his neck to tilt his head down so our foreheads touch.

Lucas wraps his arms around my waist, clutching me close as his nose brushes against mine. I hear his breathing pick up slightly as he squeezes his eyes shut. I know he's battling with himself, weighing the pros and cons.

He is so unsure of his instincts. He doesn't trust what his wolf is telling him, and it's unwise not to listen to what your wolf is telling you.

Lucas pulls back suddenly, looking at the bedroom door as it opens. I take a few steps back, crossing my arms over my chest as Travis walks over, giving me a nod.

"Alpha, Luna." Travis meets Lucas's gaze, a glare settling on his features.

Lucas frowns as he runs a hand through his hair and nods. He then walks out of the room without another word. I stare after him with confusion.

"What's going on?" I ask, looking over at Travis.

Travis shoves his hands into the pockets of his jeans, walking over to bump my arm with his elbow. "Trust your mate, Mae."

"Is he in trouble?" I ask.

"He's just going to speak with Elizabeth, the elder." My stomach drops to the floor as I begin to feel unsettled.

My wolf claws to get out. She doesn't want our mate near that woman, and neither do I.

I run out of my room quickly, sprinting down the hall, nearly jumping down the staircase as I look towards where my wolf is taking me.

I get to Lucas's office where I pause and listen to what is going on inside.

Why am I so stupid sometimes? They only communicate through mind link.

I reach for the office door when a hand clamps down on my wrist, pulling me away. I glance up to see Travis looking down at me, an eyebrow raised.

"I don't trust her," I whisper, not wanting to be caught.

"She's our elder. She's not going to hurt him." Travis growls at me with a harsh whisper.

I hate when males growl at me. It's very irritating.

"What are they saying?" I cross my arms, not accepting the fact that she isn't a part of all that has happened. Perhaps she is playing with his mind.

"She's telling Lucas that she believes he made the wrong decision and to prepare for war."

A war she will be issuing.

I let out a sigh and open the office door before Travis could stop me. Lucas and Elizabeth both look at me, but I disregard the elder as I walk to stand beside my mate. Elizabeth stares at me, her gaze skeptical. She's wondering if I'm on to her.

I am now.

"What is going on?" The question is general, but my eyes never leave Elizabeth.

She peeks over at Lucas for a quick second. "I'm just warning your mate of what might come," she says, her voice calm.

I notice her fingers twitch at her side, and that she licks her lips. Both are signs of anxiety. She's growing nervous.

"Whatever happens, we will make it through. If war comes, the outcasts will be annihilated. I'll be sure of it. No reason to fuss." I give her a smile, trying to convince her that I am on her side.

Elizabeth cocks her head to the side, arching an eyebrow. "How will you do that? You're not even the official luna yet."

She's testing me, trying to see what my breaking point is. It is unwise to question an alpha's position.

"The Shadow pack, Rose pack, and Prowler pack will fight with us. They wouldn't last five minutes." I threaten her.

I am threatening whatever is going through her mind, and I am threatening the wolves that were exiled.

Elizabeth nods. "Seems we have nothing to worry about then." Her lips twitch into a tiny smile. She looks at Lucas one last time before she turns and exits the office.

My wolf settles within me now that she is away from Lucas. I lean against the desk and watch as Lucas crosses his arms. He stares at me with a confused expression.

I honestly have no idea why I don't like that woman. From what I see, she seems to have the pack's interests and Lucas's in mind. But I can't shake what my wolf is telling me, and I will never second guess my animal instincts. They're scarcely wrong.

"I'm sorry," I whisper. "I guess I don't like other women around you." I lie, hoping to ease the tension.

Lucas gives a short laugh as he walks over and kisses my forehead.

"I want to hear you," I whisper, wrapping my arms around his neck.

Lucas frowns, pulling his eyebrows together. Perhaps that wasn't the best choice of words on my part, but I am desperate to communicate with him more simply. I hate having to find our phones and spending time typing what we think when we could just project our thoughts to one another.

I press my lips firmly against Lucas's causing him to let out a soft growl as he steps closer. I am pinned against the desk as he grips onto my hips tightly, his mouth hot against mine. My fingers dig into his hair, pulling on it slightly as I keep it prisoner in my grasp.

Lucas steps in between my legs, causing me to wrap them around his waist. He cups his hands under my butt as he picks me up. Our lips never cease attacking as Lucas takes us out of his office and up the stairs.

I am surprised at how skillfully and fluidly he walks up, never struggling with me in his arms.

I break away from the kiss and peck down his neck, my tongue licking out to taste the smooth skin at the juncture of his neck. Lucas lets out a groan as he kicks open the French doors to our room, dropping me on the bed.

I crawl back to the pillows as Lucas shuts the bedroom doors. He walks briskly over, hovering on top of me to connect his lips with mine. My breathing quickens as I understand that this is actually going to happen.

He's going to mark me. I'm going to be officially his.

Lucas kisses down my cheek, along my jaw, and my neck. I moan, arching my back as he nibbles slightly at my skin.

"Do it. Please."

I don't care that I am begging. I am desperate for him, and I am not ashamed.

Lucas's mouth opens wide before he sinks his teeth into my neck, causing me to growl and grip tightly at his shoulders. I feel warm liquid trickle down my shoulder, soaking into the bed sheets under me. His tongue flickers over the bite, gathering the blood and sealing the wound as he pulls back to look down at me.

As I stare up at him, a smile tugging at my lips, I can't help but feel completely whole at this moment. It's almost as if until this very second, I have been going through the motions but never really living. My lungs were contracting and relaxing but never really breathing in air. My heart was pumping blood but never truly beating.

Time to finally hear him. To hear my mate.

I open my mind to Lucas, letting every thought of the pack and of him seep into my brain. It takes a moment for me to process everything, causing an excruciating headache along the way. But it all finally clears, and I can hear him.

You're beautiful, mo grá (my love).

I am not sure if it's my idea of a perfect voice or if this is how Lucas actually sounds, but I nearly melted at his voice. His tone is husky; however, it's like honey. It sends chills down my spine, causing me to shiver.

"I love your voice," I whisper.

Lucas smiles, leaning down to give me a quick kiss. *Now, tá tú mianach. (Now, you are mine)*

Eight

Mae

September 28, 2036

I've been with the Cipher pack for two weeks now.

A lot has happened in those two weeks. Lucas drove off half of the pack; he marked me; I became the official luna; we had a ceremony and celebration, and we've even had a run in with a small rogue pack.

One thing that did not happen is mating with Lucas. I was certain our mating would be completed after the luna ceremony, but Lucas wasn't ready.

When we mate, it will be on our own time, when we're ready, not when we're "supposed" to be mated. It doesn't feel natural to me.

I have to admit that the thought is pretty attractive and romantic.

I am currently sitting at the breakfast bar, watching as Lucas whips us up a batch of pancakes. He is very confident of himself in the kitchen and knows exactly where everything is. He doesn't read the recipe, and it seems that he knows the right measurements for the ingredients, and while that scares me slightly, I am still impressed he cooks his own breakfast.

Travis and Jake enter the kitchen, throwing punches at each other. I watch with amusement as Jake is thrown into a kitchen chair, causing it to break at impact. I hear a growl as Lucas drops a plate of pancakes in front of me and marches over to pick Jake up by the scruff of his shirt.

Travis and Jake have become my good friends. They act like the older brothers I never had. They play video games with me, and they also protect me. They sit with me at breakfast and share obscene and sarcastic jokes with me, but then they treat me with the utmost respect.

Lisa has also been a good friend. She reminds me much of Aunt Natalie with her high spirit and her gleaming expressions. She is happy with Travis, and it shows as she walks around the house with a purpose. Lisa has been my source of gossip. She always has my ear when she gives the juicy details about dramatic teenage fights or what the next course of action is against the rogues.

You guys are such children. Lucas snaps in the mind link.

Travis is laughing his butt off, doubling over and gripping the table for support as Jake gets shoved out of the house. Lucas then returns to push Travis out as well.

I can hear him laughing even when the back door is shut.

"I liked that table set," I whisper mostly to myself as I stare at the black and brown handcrafted wooden chair lying in pieces on the ground. The chairs and tables are made of oak and stained with dark brown and black color.

Lucas stands across from me, leaning on the counter as he drowns our pancakes with syrup. Just how I like them.

We both eat from the giant stack, making our way through until we meet at the middle. I am completely full, allowing Lucas to finish off the last few bites. He then discards the plate and forks into the sink and walks over to stand behind me.

Lucas flicks the hair off my shoulder and nuzzles into the crook of my neck, giving my mark a faint kiss. Fire erupts all over my body as I lean against him, moaning.

"Will you do something for me?" I ask.

Lucas kisses along my shoulder and back up to my jaw, nibbling on my ear.

Anything, he whispers in my head.

I close my eyes, trying to focus on what I wanted to ask him, but his lips are so distracting.

"Will you teach me—" I am cut off when he bites down at my skin gently, causing me to gasp.

I jump off the stool and turn to face Lucas, holding a hand out to keep him from advancing to me. His eyes dance with amusement.

"How to speak your language?" I finish.

You want to learn how to speak Gaelic?

"Well, don't I have to? The Cipher pack communicates in Gaelic, does it not?"

Lucas nods slowly, staring at me intensely as a smile plays on his lips. He's going to be the death of me.

A dhéanann tú Fuaimeanna greannmhar nuair codlata agat.

I stare at Lucas with my mouth hanging open as his beautiful language washes over me. He spoke so fast that it sounded gibberish. Did he actually form a sentence, or did he just throw in grunts and murmurs?

"What?" I ask.

You start now. First lesson: figure out what I just said. Then we can move on.

I scrunch my eyebrows together at what he is saying. How on earth am I supposed to know what he said? I don't understand anything besides 'my love' or 'my brown one.' And that didn't sound remotely similar to those two phrases.

"Luc, that's not fair," I grumble, and he just shrugs his shoulders, smirking like a kid. "I'm never going to figure it out."

That's alright. You have until you die to figure it out, mo cheann dunn. It rests in your hands. Lucas gives my forehead a kiss before he turns and walks away.

I feel my heart race as anger and annoyance overcomes me. How could he just throw me that sentence and expect me to decipher it without so much as little help? I take out my cell phone and open up Google Translate, switching the language to Gaelic. My thumbs hover at the screen as I try to remember what exactly it was he said.

I remember what he said. Gibberish.

How can I figure it out when I don't even know how to spell it or enunciate it?

"This is horseshit." *Forgive my language, Father, Mother, Aunt Natalie, Uncle Trent, Moon Goddess, and so on.*

I storm outside, determined to find Travis and Jake. Of course, they didn't get far, tussling on the grass. Sensing me, they look up from being entangled in each other's death grips.

"Luna! How do you do?" Jake groans out, pushing Travis off him. Jake gets to his feet, dusting himself off.

"I need your help," I say.

Travis quickly gets to his feet as well, crossing his arms as all traces of playfulness leave his features.

"I need to figure out what"—since I couldn't pronounce it, I project my memory of Lucas's voice to them—"means."

Travis and Jake burst out laughing, causing me to stare at them in utter shock. I knew it was gibberish!

"Oh. I love that guy," Travis says, clearly referring to Lucas. "It means—" He suddenly stops, his spine straightening and his eyes become unfocused.

No, no, no, no! He's cheating!

"I'm sorry, Luna. But we've been informed we can't help you," Jake says, a smile still on his face.

I squint at them. That alpha won't know what hit him. Seeing that I have to figure it out on my own, I turn and walk back into the house, heading to Lucas's office. I push open the doors and march over to his desk. Lucas stares at me with a small smile, but I ignore him. I grab the back of his chair and pull it away from the desk, taking its place.

Leaning over the computer, I bring up Google Translate and try to spell out what Lucas said to me. It's so hard to type a language you don't understand. When you think it starts with an "s," the word actually begins with a "t."

Like tsunami! That's how it is but with all of their words.

Lucas chuckles behind me, causing me to tighten the muscles in my back.

He's playing tricks with your mind. Don't give in. Letting out a gust of breath, I stand up straight and calmly walk out of his office, determined to speak with Lisa.

I'm sorry, mo ghrá. But I have complete faith in you. Otherwise, I wouldn't have given you this challenge.

Even though Lucas's words cause a smile to stretch across my face, I am still giving him the silent treatment. I won't speak to him until I have figured this out.

Once I get to Lisa and Travis's room, I knock on the door. Lisa invites me in, and I walk over to sit beside her on the couch she has tucked to the side of the room around a coffee table.

"Hi, Mae. You look ravishing today."

"Oh, do I?" I give her a frown, causing her to laugh.

"I heard about what Lucas is doing to you. It has to be done to every new member of the pack if they don't know Gaelic. However, I find this one quite funny." Lisa chuckles.

I narrow my eyes. Everyone knows what he said. What if it's embarrassing?

Was he speaking about the time I fell down the stairs and broke my arm?

"Please, help me…It's killing me." I beg Lisa.

She laughs, shaking her head. "I can't, Mae. It won't be genuine, and you won't feel accomplished."

I bite my bottom lip. Yes, she is right. I won't feel that I actually finished the challenge if I get help from someone else. I have to do it on my own.

I take out my phone and go back to Google Translate. Lisa moves beside me as I try to type in the words. She would occasionally cough obnoxiously if I spelled the word wrong. Even with her "helping" me, I grow frustrated. I want to chuck my phone across the room and scream.

I crack a few words, such as sleep and you. I glance over at Lisa and ask, "He's talking about me sleeping?"

Lisa smirks softly, and I feel my eyes widen.

Deciding to take a different approach, I type in English words to see if I can get the translation. I type in "you sleep" and then just stare…What can he be saying about me? What do I do when I sleep?

I try a few different phrases, checking to see if they will work. They don't…The only words that seem familiar are "when you sleep."

What when I sleep?

What do I do when I sleep?

I suddenly remember a conversation that I had with Aunt Natalie a while back.

* * *

"*You are a monster when you're asleep,*" *Aunt Natalie says when I enter the dinette.*

I arch an eyebrow at her as I sit next to her at the table.

"*What do you mean?*" *I ask, scratching the nest of hair atop my head.*

Natalie's eyes watch me as she takes in my ragged appearance. I toss and turn in bed, and my clothes sometimes end up backward or even on the floor…So what?

"*I mean, you speak…Or at least you try to. It's mostly grunts and whimpers.*"

"*What? You're saying I make sounds when I'm sleeping?*"

Uncle Mason walks in, ruffling my hair as he takes a seat at the table as well, just making a bad situation (my hair) worse.

"*Funny sounds. Like you're having se—Ow!*" *Mason screams when Natalie slaps him in the arm.*

* * *

Oh no.

I quickly type in the phrase I have running through my mind, and of course, it's a match.

He's dead.

I pocket my phone and sprint down the stairs as Lisa laughs her butt off upstairs. I throw open Lucas's doors, causing him to look up at me with wide eyes.

I run over and jump onto his lap, futilely punching his chest as he just chuckles, wrapping an arm around me.

"You make funny noises when you sleep!"

A wide smile cracks across Lucas's face. *Well done, mo cheann donn. Are you ready to begin your lessons?*

I cease my attack and sit back on his lap, looking down at him. Lucas reaches up and tucks a lock of hair behind my ear.

"I am ready, *mo grhá.*"

Nine

Mae

October 1, 2036

Lucas has been a wonderful teacher. He is patient and doesn't get frustrated even when I become agitated.

His language is hard to learn. It is so different from the English language, and none of the Gaelic words sound like English.

In Spanish, some of the words sound similar to the English translation, such as *teléfono*, which means a telephone, or *lámpara*, which means lamp. But with Gaelic, there are no similarities. Even though I find Lucas's language beautiful, I can't help but think he is making up words just to mess with me.

I am currently sitting in Lucas's office, working on my studies as Lucas attends to some pack business. He doesn't seem to mind having me in the room, and it gives me comfort to be beside him. We are hardly apart from one another.

I peek up to stare at Lucas. His big brown eyes read over a document placed on his desk, head resting on his right hand. His fingers subconsciously rub away the stress that is gathering at his forehead, and his lips are pressed together.

"What is it you are reading?" I ask.

I have to name all of the members of the pack that left...to legalize their separation so they can create a new pack. I am ashamed to say it, but I don't know any of their names, Lucas says, not looking up from the paper.

Standing, I walk over to stand behind him, gazing down at a paper that holds two names. He only remembers two people out of a hundred or so who betrayed him.

I wrap my arms around him, placing my hands on his chest as I rest my chin on his shoulder. "Look at the pack registry. You remember the ones loyal to you...So cross them off, and the ones remaining are the ones who left." I suggest, shrugging my shoulders.

Sure, that would take a long time, but I see that he has no other way to remember the names.

You're brilliant. Lucas grabs my left hand off his chest and places a soft kiss to the inside of my wrist. *This is why I am so lucky to have you.*

"Hmm, yes. That…among many other reasons." I place a kiss on his cheek and head back over to sit on the couch again, returning to my studies.

Sea, mar shampla an bhfíric go bhfuil tú tóin álainn.

I whip around and glare at him. "What about my bottom?" I ask.

Lucas gives me a large grin as he crossed his arms. *You only got bottom out of that?*

"I made sure to learn the inappropriate words first, so I know if you're saying anything…well, inappropriate."

Lucas laughs, his light brown eyes, for the first time, shining with joy.

Seeing him so happy makes me proud. It is an accomplishment to make Lucas smile and laugh. I know he has been through so much in his life, so to know that I am the reason he is happy fills me with pride.

"What exactly did you say?"

I said, "Yes, for example, the fact you have a beautiful bottom."

I look down at my butt and smile. "Classy," I mumble and sit on the couch, looking down at the Gaelic books given to me by Lucas.

Yes, I have homework. I haven't had homework since I was sixteen years old. In packs, our education is different. We learn the basics, such as mathematics, science, and history. But we also learn about werewolf history, the ways of pack life, and the different roles the members might have in a pack. At the age of sixteen, we graduate school.

I hate having homework again. I was so used to the freedom of never having to worry about it. But now I have a workbook to help me learn Gaelic. Sure, this is something I want to understand, but that doesn't take away the fact that I feel as though I'm in school again.

Tá sé seo dúr. (This is stupid), I say, probably butchering the phrase.

Lucas chuckles. *Why don't you take a break?*

I don't hesitate to slap the books close and pull out my phone, bringing up my mom's number. I send her a quick text asking how everyone is doing. I haven't been in much contact with my family, and I feel sort of guilty. I was always close to them and never imagined my life without them. However, living with Lucas and taking on some of the responsibilities within the Cipher pack has proven to be a pretty enjoyable life. I can see myself soon falling in love with Lucas.

I peek up through my lashes as he crosses names off a copy of the pack registry, smirking at the fact that he followed my advice. Lucas's jaw is set as his eyes travel across the paper, and I can nearly see the gears turning in his head as he tries to remember everyone. A lock of blond hair falls across his forehead, causing him to shake it to the side before he hangs his head into his hands.

I am about to ask if he is alright when my phone starts vibrating in my hand. I glance down to see my mom's picture and name lighting up my phone. I smile, biting my bottom lip as I answer and hold it to my ear. "Hi, Mom."

"So, you are alive!"

I roll my eyes at her sarcasm. I hear fumbling before Aunt Natalie and Uncle Mason are yelling into my ear.

"Mae! There better be a good explanation as to why you are just contacting us now!" Aunt Natalie hollers.

"Squirt, if you don't check in, you'll force us to go and retrieve you." Uncle Mason threatens.

A stupid smile spreads across my face as I curl up on the couch and close my eyes, listening to them fuss and argue about who gets to hold the phone.

"Did you not hear what I said?" Mason asks.

"I heard you. Just keep talking. Tell me what's going on."

Mason, Natalie, and my mom don't fail to fill me in with every detail of every second. Hearing them talk about the pack and everything that is happening without me tears my heart. I never really knew how much I miss all of them until I realize that I am no longer a member of the Shadow pack. I am the luna of the Cipher pack now.

Tears roll down my cheeks as I hear my father yell something at Mason about not letting him know I was on the phone.

"Hey, baby girl." My dad's deep yet gentle voice fills my ears.

I let out a sigh and smirk slightly. "Hi, Daddy. How have you been?"

"Exhausted. The Prowler pack is being a pain in my ass."

"Landon!" I hear my mom yell before I hear a thump, and I smile, knowing she just punched his arm for swearing.

"I'm sorry, dear." I can practically hear my father's eyes rolling in their sockets. "Anyway, the Prowler pack has been abandoning its duties. They aren't taking their patrol shifts, causing the Shadow pack and the Rose pack to work double. They are also refraining from communicating. We hardly see Jenny anymore."

I frown. That doesn't sound like Jenny. I run a hand through my hair as I stare up at the ceiling.

"Well, all you can do is voice your warning. You tell them if they don't participate in the treaty, then it will be broken. I admit, it is disheartening considering I used the Prowler pack to threaten someone, but if you can't trust them, cut them loose before you go down with them," I say.

"I'm proud of you, Mae." I was about to ask if that was another test before he interrupts me. "Why did you threaten someone?"

"I needed to ensure the loyalty of a pack member. Not a big issue." I shrug even though he can't see it. Talking to my father is so calming; I wish we could talk for hours, but I know he has tasks to return to. "I love you, Dad. Tell everyone, especially Mom, that I love them."

Tears gather again as I know the conversation is coming to a close.

"I love you, sweet pea." He hangs up, and I let out an exasperated sigh as I roll onto my side.

My eyes focus on a piece of string that came loose on the couch. I pick at it, twirling it around my finger as I lightly tug it. My stomach churns, almost causing me to throw up, but I know that isn't the issue.

I am homesick, and I miss my family.

Two warm fingers brush against my cheek, gently gathering the tears. I look up to see Lucas squatting in front of me, a frown on his lips.

I hate seeing you sad, mo ghrá. You're not a prisoner here. You can see your family whenever you wish it. Lucas offers a small smile as his fingers continue to caress my face.

My duties come before my feelings. I have to make sure that everything with the Cipher pack is settled before I take a mini-vacation. I won't leave Lucas here alone, not when the rogues who abandoned us could strike.

I reach over and run my fingers through his soft hair, giving it a gentle tug, pulling him closer to me. Lucas ducks his head down slightly and gives me a short and sweet kiss. My toes curl against the couch. I shift, sitting up, so Lucas is now kneeling between my legs. I deepen the kiss, nibbling on his bottom lip as passion takes over.

Lucas wraps his arms around me, pulling me close, so I wrap my legs around his waist, moaning at how delicious he tastes. He pulls back slightly to kiss down my neck, suckling on my mark. I throw my head back and groan, tangling my hands in his hair, keeping him prisoner. He is killing me.

I lean forward and attack his neck as well, leaving him love bites that will most definitely be visible for a few days. Or weeks. But he doesn't seem to mind.

"I want you," I whisper against the soft skin at his shoulder.

Just like that, it is as if a bucket of ice water is dumped over Lucas. He freezes in my embrace, growing tense as he dislodges himself from me. I watch as he sits back on his feet, running a hand through his hair.

Ní gá duit a chiallaíonn go. Ní mian leat go. (You do not mean that. You do not want that.)

I squint at him. Why is he speaking his language when he knows I don't understand yet. Although, I do know he's not talking about my breasts or butt...

I bite my bottom lip, shaking my head at him.

"I-I don't...I don't know—" I stumble, not being able to hide the rejection that is overwhelming me.

Even though I don't know what he said, I do know what he means.

He doesn't want this. He still doesn't want this. After everything, he still doesn't want me. Lucas gets to his feet, looking down at me with furrowed brows. His face is hard, yet his eyes show so much pain and sorrow. I want to know what he is thinking. When I try to tap into his mind, I find he has his walls up.

Why?

Lucas shakes his head. *Ag dul duit sin i bhfad níos fearr. (You deserve so much better.)*

Without another word, he turns on his heel and walks out of the room. I watch after him. What have I done wrong? Why would he just leave after such an affectionate moment? I thought we were finally getting somewhere, and now we are back at the campgrounds where he nearly ordered me to reject him.

Too late for that, baby. You marked me. You're stuck with me.

Ten

Mae

October 1, 2036

After Lucas walked out of the office, I went online and Google what he said to me. *That little idiot, he is as dramatic as a teenage girl...*

Every teenage girl besides me. I'm not dramatic. I think to myself and ignore the irony of it.

I storm out of his office, jogging to the kitchen where I see him standing at the fridge. He is bent forward, reaching for a water bottle on the bottom shelf. Once he closes the door, I grab his shirt and shove his back against the fridge. He looks down at me with wide eyes.

"You do not tell me what I do and don't want. I will be the judge of what I desire. And what I want is you. And don't ever say I deserve better." I reach up, resting my hands on his cheeks, looking dead into his eyes so he knows I'm telling the truth. "There is no one better for me than you."

Lucas stares at me for a moment before he nods and reaches up to tuck a piece of hair behind my ear.

I just don't want you to be forever bound to me, for you to then later realize that I am not good enough.

"Well, too damn late. I bear your mark, and unless someone cuts it off or burns it off, I am yours until I die. So live with it, *dathúil*." I arch my eyebrow as I watch his reaction. Either I said exactly what I meant or I just majorly insulted him.

Really? Handsome? You're learning fast.

I shrug. "Not really. I looked up a few words so I can give you a couple nicknames as well. But I still needed Google's help to figure out what you said earlier," I mumble, grabbing the water from his hand, unscrewing it to take a long swig.

"Lovebirds, move." I look over to see Travis standing at the kitchen's entrance with his arms crossed. "Either make me a sandwich or move."

I glare at him, taking a step away from the fridge. "What's up your butt this morning?'

"I am listening to the internal battle going on with this one"—he jerks a thumb over to Lucas —"and I have to listen to you butcher our language."

My mouth gapes open at how incredibly rude he is being. Travis has never said anything so harsh before. He is usually so supportive when it comes to me learning the language.

When I catch the smirk on his face, I realize he is only joking. I punch his back softly.

"You're such a jerk." I growl, crossing my arms as he steps back from the fridge with turkey, ham, lettuce, mayo, mustard, and onions in his hands.

Travis dumps the contents onto the counter and grabs the bread from a basket, which is tucked in the corner of the kitchen. He begins lathering the bread with mayo.

"*Mé díreach nach bhfuil in ann a smaoineamh i bhfad le do yapping tairiseach.* (I just can't think much with your constant yapping.)"

Lucas reaches over and thumps Travis on the back of the head, growling lowly at him.

I scrunch my lips to the side, trying to figure out what Travis said to me. "Constant yapping?"

Travis smiles, shaking his head as I notice Lucas is giving him a private message. I watch as they communicate. Travis always has a happy, dorky smile on his face as Lucas glares and frowns.

"What did he say?"

Nothing. Lucas barks.

I stare at him with my right eyebrow quirked upward.

"Don't be short with me."

Travis takes a bite of his sandwich, his eyes taking in everything.

"If you insulted me, you better be aware that I will soon be able to understand what you are saying, *gránna* (ugly)."

Travis gasps, placing a hand over his wounded heart. "I am beautiful." He reaches his hand up to flip his imaginary hair as he turns and walks out, swaying his hips from side to side.

I laugh after him, leaning into Lucas's side, wrapping an arm around his waist.

I'm going to go work some more on the pack registry. Why don't you go see what Travis and Jake are doing? Or Lisa? Lucas places a kiss on the side of my head before pulling away and heading to the office.

I stare after him, raising my arms at my side before I slap my hands to the outside of my thighs. What was that?

He just needs space, I tell myself.

So I decide to do as he says and look for Travis and Jake. Maybe they will lighten the mood.

I run up the stairs and enter the game room where I see only Jake sitting on a beanbag chair, playing Call of Duty. I walk over and plop down beside him.

"Where's Travis?" I ask, grabbing a controller and turning it on.

"With Lisa," Jake says, smiling over at me.

Of course. They are obsessed with each other.

Jake restarts the Xbox and sets up a game so we can both play. "Do you know how this game goes?" he asks, raising his eyebrows at me.

I reach over and thump him on the shoulder. "I don't live under a rock." I laugh, and Jake shakes his head. "Prepare to get your butt whipped by a girl!"

Jake chuckles. "You're on, Matthews!"

He sets us up on a zombie game, our map being an abandoned theater. Even though we're on the same team, we determine who is better by the number of kills, headshots, and overall points given.

Together, we get to level twenty, the farthest I have ever gotten. I usually play this game by myself, and it is hard to get very far when you have to kill all these zombies yourself. But with Jake, we were a great team. We had each other's back, and if either one of us is down, we risk our lives to revive each other.

After the first round, I am proclaimed the winner. I can't help but boast and brag, immediately causing him to call for a rematch.

Jake wins the second round. So of course, we have to play again to break the tie. It gets a little rambunctious. We try to sabotage each other; stealing each other's controllers or reaching over and pressing random buttons as zombies swarm us.

I am extremely competitive. I hate losing, especially when it comes to games. And apparently, Jake is the same way. His face gets red as he concentrates solely on the game. Even a rogue attack can't divert his attention. I laugh, knifing another zombie in the head when Jake gets wounded.

"Crap!" He growls, looking over at me. "Revive me!"

I hesitate. Shouldn't I just let him die? Then I would win? But we were on level twenty-one, the furthest so far. I want to see how far we can go.

"Mae!" Jake grows frustrated, causing me to grumble as I kill a few more zombies and make my way over to Jake's wounded character who is lying on the ground.

I revive him as he shoots any zombies who walk behind me. Once he is healed, we return to killing every other zombie on the level. As level twenty-two comes to play, I am overwhelmed with how much harder it is.

When I go down, I wait for Jake to come to revive me; however, he doesn't make a move to come help.

"Are you going to revive me?" I ask.

A stupid smirk crosses Jake's face, and I gasp. He's just going to let me die after I saved him? I leap over and tackle him to the ground, struggling to grasp his controller as he fights against me. Jake rolls, pinning me to the ground as he sits on my hips, yanking the controller from my grasp as he kills a zombie and I die.

"Yes!" He cheers as he is declared a winner.

I glare up at him, shoving him off me. "You cheated!" I snarl, grabbing the collar of his shirt, throwing him to the ground.

Jake just laughs, his eyes closing as he just shakes with laughter underneath me.

I pound on his chest. "Best three out of five!" I get up, sitting back on the beanbag chair, controller in hand. "Let's go!" I demand.

Jake gets to his feet and walks over, patting my head as he passes. I turn to see him making his way to the door.

"No!" I jump up, sprinting over to jump on his back. "You are playing again! I refuse to lose!"

Jake grabs my arm that is around his neck, flipping me over his shoulder, so I hit the ground with a thud. I grunt as he wraps a hand around my neck, holding me down as he looks down at me with a smile.

"Give it up, baby. You lost. You're a loser. You may now call me the Zombie King."

I sneer up at him, thrashing against his hold, but he doesn't let up. "Zombie King, my booty," I growl.

I punch and kick at him; however, he doesn't release me. Not until I calm down. I lie still on the ground, my breathing frantic as I raise my eyebrows at him. He can let me go now. Jake's bright green eyes stare down at me, a warmth swarming within them. I feel my heart squeeze tight as I see his face inching closer to mine.

What is he doing?

His lips brush mine, causing me to snarl and shove him off. "Wha—"

I am cut off by a deep growl. I freeze, my heart stopping as I feel dread and guilt wash over me. Lucas's voice resounds within my mind.

What the hell is going on?

Eleven

Lucas

October 1, 2036

    I shut my office door, leaning against it as my heart races and head reels. I don't understand what she sees and what she is so stubborn about.
    Does she not see my countless flaws?
    I am not fit to run this pack. I just lost half of them, and soon, I will lose even more. It is just a matter of time before the ones loyal to me will see what set the other wolves off.
    I have been trying my hardest to understand the ways of an alpha, but I was never taught them. It isn't something you can just pick up. It is a lifelong commitment

with years of studying. It is a job, a duty where I have to take care and ensure the safety of hundreds.

I am broken. I have watched the Rogue Massacre with my own eyes. I saw my father getting murdered. I saw the desperation in his eyes as he silently pleaded me to run the other way. One cannot describe the pain that comes from seeing the weakness and the sadness that my father held during his last moments. I held his lifeless body in my arms, and all I could think about was that his last thought was how I disobeyed his last wish. I disappointed him, even as he died.

Then, there was Gavin. He was my best friend. He was four years older than me; however, the age difference was unnoticeable. Gavin took me everywhere other than when he was having alpha lessons with our father. I chose not to go, which I am now regretting. I would have benefited from the lessons. I should have been responsible enough to go. Gavin would stay up late nights to play video games with me even if he had to get up at the crack of dawn the next morning to run patrol. He never complained. He was always there for me—when I broke my leg from falling out of a tree, or when Travis punched me in the face over action figures. Gavin would put Travis in his place and then put a meaty steak over my bruising eye.

I miss him the most.

Lastly, there is also the fact that I can't speak. Speaking through the mind link is much easier than communicating through our phones; however, it exhausts me. I not only have to produce the thought, but I have to transfer it towards Mae. I have to break through her mind and find her deepest thoughts to project what I am thinking, and when I get exhausted, I get frustrated and short-tempered, which is something Mae is starting to notice. She even scolded me for being short with her today.

    I smile at the memory.

    She is such a spitfire. She speaks whatever is on her mind, not worried about the consequences.

    I take a seat at my desk and take out the registry again, working on remembering who all stayed at my side.

    As I work, I can hear Mae yelling profanities at Jake. I assume that they're playing Call of Duty. With her competitive nature, I feel bad for Jake. He better let her win if he wants to walk away with all of his body parts.

    Crossing off the last name on the registry, I look down to see the remaining ones. I curl my lips in disgust at the names of the men who left, who were disloyal, and who hurt Mae.

    I begin transferring their names to a different paper, officially writing them off as rogues. Hopefully, they will be killed off one by one. Suddenly, a loud thump sounds from upstairs. I lift my head, smirking as I hear Jake laughing as Mae screams at him for not reviving her. I am glad she has found a friend in him. She needs someone to keep her company while I am working. It can't be fun for her to constantly be sitting in my office in silence.

    Once I am done with the list, I stand from my desk and decide to go see how badly injured Jake is. He may need to visit the pack doctor.

    Taking the stairs two at a time, I reach the third floor in seconds and walk into the game room where I peek in to see Mae and Jake lying on the floor. Jake hovers over Mae as she has her hand on his chest. I see Jake lick his lips, causing me to growl.

They kiss.

My heart seems to tear in half as I witness this. How can she do this to me? Has she finally realized that Jake is a better match for her? That I am not worth her time?

What the hell is going on?

* * *

Mae

Jake jumps up to his feet, holding his hands up as he stares at Lucas with wide eyes. I get to my feet as well, stepping back.

I have never seen someone so terrified, and I have never seen someone so angered, either.

As I watch Lucas glaring down at his friend, I try to convince myself that he isn't going to hurt him. Jake is a very good friend of Lucas. He just had a lapse in his judgment.

"It's not—"

Jake is cut off by a fist to the jaw. He spirals to the ground, causing me to jump back, gasping. Lucas seethes with raw anger as he looks over at me. His expression is nothing but betrayal and hatred.

I knew it was only a matter of time. But with my friend? He snarls at me.

My mouth gapes open as I am thrown back by his allegation. I wasn't the one who made a move. Why is he blaming me?

"No, Lucas it wasn't——-"

I don't get to reply because I am grabbed by the arm in a vice grip. I watch with wide eyes as he yanks me from the room, dragging me towards our bedroom. He throws me in and locks the door, standing in front of me with crossed arms.

I actually believed you. Lucas's "voice" cracks. Even though it is only a thought, I can still hear the pain behind it.

"I-I—We…It's not what you think!" I stammer.

I have never been so incoherent. I never let anyone have control over me; however, Lucas's pain is weighing down on me like a thousand bricks. I can't think clearly with all his emotions.

"I didn't want that! We were just playing a game. It just got too far! He wasn't thinking—"

"No!"

I lean back when the word leaves his lips. Lucas snarls, lip curling over his teeth.

Did he just speak?

I feel my heart race as I quickly close my eyes and absorb the sound. His voice is deep and scratchy. It is evident it hasn't been used for a very long time. He couldn't control the pitch or the volume, but that didn't matter. It was the most beautiful thing I have ever heard.

A smile plays on my lips. My Lucas just spoke.

"How is that possible?" I whisper, mostly to myself. When I open my eyes, I see Lucas staring at me with a blank expression.

Why do you care?

I sigh.

"Why are you so dramatic?" I ask as I walk towards him, ignoring his threatening growl and the step he takes backward. I shove his back into the door, just as I had with the fridge earlier this morning. "I have told you time and again and I will continue to tell you until you understand. I don't want anyone other than you. You marked me. I am yours, soul, body, heart…just as you are mine." I reach up and place a kiss to the crook of his neck.

Lucas tenses around me as I feel my canines elongate. They scrape across his skin, teasing before I wrap my arms around his waist, my hands in between his shoulder blades and the door. I don't wait any longer, and I do what I have been dying to do since Lucas marked me.

I mark him.

My mother did it to my father. It was an intimate act that seemed so right between them. The female marking the male is rare, but apparently, it's not with my family.

Lucas moans, gripping the back of my shirt, holding tight as I complete the process. Pulling back to wipe the blood from my lips, I smirk, proud of the mark on his shoulder.

"You are mine, Lucas Donovan. The only man I will ever love." I run my fingers through his soft hair as he stares down at me with his beautiful doe eyes.

I love you, he whispers in my mind, resting his forehead against mine. *I planned to tell you tonight. That's why I was so angry. I just realized my love for you and you were kissing—*

I place a hand over his lips even though that does nothing to keep him from talking.

"No. Never. I'll never kiss anyone but you." I promise.

Lucas pulls me into a hug, burying his face into my shoulder as he clings to me. I close my eyes, happy that I was able to finally make clear how much Lucas means to me. I will never want more than him.

There is no one better than Lucas.

I grunt, Lucas mutters in my head.

I pull back, eyebrows scrunched together as I stare up at him.

I can moan, grunt, and laugh. I didn't say no. I just modified my grunt into a 'no.' It's easy to do it with small words, something short and quick. 'No,' 'okay,' 'go,' 'you'...Travis helped me a while ago to learn how to do it.

I stare up at him in awe. Does he not see how much of an accomplishment that is? Whether he wants to believe it or not, he spoke. Even if he was told that he would never speak again, he spoke. And I don't care if it was because he was yelling at me. In fact, I'll let him yell at me whenever he wishes if that will cause him to speak.

"Lucas, that is amazing. Why haven't you told me?"

It's not as though I can have a conversation with you. It kills me that I can never speak to you with my actual voice. I want to tell you how beautiful you are, to whisper endearments against your lips as *we kiss, and to actually say our wedding vows out loud...*Lucas frowns, shaking his head.

Tears gather in my eyes as he says this. I have never thought of it that way.

"It doesn't matter," I say.

Yes—

"No, Lucas. It doesn't. Because when we get married, you will say the vows out loud. If it's something that you want, then I will help you. I will find someone to operate on your vocal cords. I will even give half of mine to you. You will speak again. I promise. I will make sure that you will speak again." I reach up, brushing hair out of his face. "I love you, Lucas, and I will ensure your happiness."

Lucas presses me close to him. *I'm pretty sure it's supposed to be the other way around. I should be making sacrifices for* you.

"We're a team now. We make sacrifices for each other."

Twelve

Mae

October 10, 2036

    I pick and play with my pancakes, staring down at the delectable breakfast; however, I didn't have the appetite to eat it, which is odd because I usually eat five of them.

    Lisa is already finishing her third when she looks over to see I have barely made a dent on my first.

    "Are you okay?" she asks.

    I lift my eyes to give her a soft smile and nod. For some reason, I am awfully glum today. There is no reason for me to be. My life here is fantastic. I can pretty much understand what everyone is saying with the Gaelic tongue. It is just hard to say what I want back to them.

Lucas is great. He has been the ever loving, endearing mate that I am proud to have. He officially ruled the traitors as rogues, naming them a threat to all other packs. They will never be accepted in a pack. They may create their own, but it will be against the werewolf laws.

Jake never made a move on me again. He profusely apologized to both Lucas and me, claiming it was just a mistake and that he wasn't thinking clearly. I forgave him; however, Lucas is still punishing him. Poor Jake has been running twice the amount of patrols.

Travis is still an idiot.

Lisa has become my best friend. She seems to understand me more than anyone, apart from Lucas. Just looking at me, she can guess my mood, my health. For instance, she knows right away when my time of the month is. She even made a point to Travis to watch his attitude around me, knowing just how short my fuse is.

"Are wu gonna finsh tha?" Travis asks with a full mouth.

I stare at him as he has half of his pancake in his mouth at a time. He struggles to chew on it, but his eyes dart to my plate, looking hopeful. I slide my plate over to him.

Still an idiot.

"What's wrong?" Lisa asks.

Lucas, who is sitting on my other side, looks up to check on me. I turn to look at Lisa, making sure Lucas doesn't see what I mouth to her.

Help me?

She nods quickly before she shoots to her feet, sliding her plate of two pancakes over to Travis whose eyes light up. He grabs the plate and dumps the food onto his own, growling with excitement as he devours our food.

I watch him for a moment before I turn and walk out of the kitchen, Lisa hot on my tail. We head up the stairs towards my bedroom where Lisa locks the door behind her.

"What's up, Duckling?"

I cringe. I don't understand how she came up with that name, but she's been calling me 'Duckling' for quite some time now.

"First, enough with that name."

Lisa smirks devilishly at me. She's never going to stop.

"Second, I honestly have no idea what is wrong. I mean, everything is fine. Everything is great. I just feel like I want to cry and scream, and when I look at Lucas, I feel like I want to jump his bones."

Lisa sits on my bed, looking at me for a moment, her eyes taking in my twitching hands, my shifty stance, and my sweating brow.

I feel as if I'm anxious about something...But what is there to be anxious about? As far as I know, there is nothing planned to look forward to or be nervous about.

"Hmm, yep," Lisa mutters, looking me dead in the eye. "You're in heat."

I feel my mouth drop open as I stare at her.

Instantly, I feel stupid. I want to slap myself in the face. How can I be so dumb? Of course, this is the heat. My mom has told me many lovely stories about the uncontrollable urge to have sex with your mate everywhere and anywhere.

I gulp, looking down at my hands. I'm anxious to sexually attack my mate. But I can't. Lucas made it abundantly clear that he doesn't want to mate until the right time. When is the right time?

"What do I do?" I ask.

Lisa arches her brow. "Make love to your mate?"

That's right. Everyone believes we finished the mating process the night of the Luna Ceremony.

I gnaw on my bottom lip as I wring my hands together.

"Shut up!" Lisa screams.

I jump slightly. "I didn't say anything..."

"You're a virgin?"

My eyes widen as I leap forward, trying to cover her mouth before she can say the last word, but it was too late. I am sure Travis and Lucas heard everything.

"How? There is no way...I see you two together. You practically have sex every time you look at each other."

Please kill me.

I drop my head into my hands in utter embarrassment. Lisa starts laughing her ass off, falling back on the bed.

"I can't believe you're still a virgin. Oh my goddess, that is just too funny. Lucas is gay, isn't he?"

I reach over and slap Lisa's arm, causing her to laugh again.

"No! You're so immature! We just wanted to wait," I say, crossing my arms as Lisa seems to accept this.

She nods, sitting up. "Alright. Fine. So you're a virgin in heat. Unless you want to complete the mating, you need to keep away from Lucas for the next few days."

My heart drops. Stay away? We're hardly away from each other's side. I follow him around like a lost puppy. Mostly because I feel useful when I help him with pack matters.

What am I to do for the next few days?

"This is going to be hard," I say.

"It only gets worse as the days go on too," Lisa whispers mostly to herself, and I turn my head to glare at her. "Sorry." She smirks.

I get to my feet and walk to the door.

"What are you doing? You're supposed to stay away from Lucas, not run into his arms," Lisa says pointedly.

I ignore her, opening the door and jogging down the stairs to see Lucas and Travis still sitting at the table with their empty plates. I have to speak to Lucas before Travis drags his fat ass around all day. Except he's not fat.

I come to a stop in front of Lucas, listening to Travis snickering to himself.

"If you come near me or even speak my name, I swear you will be severely punished. So if you want this whole wait-until-the-right-time thing to stay in effect, you need to keep yourself at a distance."

Lucas just stares at me, a small smirk playing on his lips. *You smell ravishing...* He inhales, closing his eyes.

I slap his arm. "Lucas Donovan! I am serious! You'll have to sleep in the guest bedroom."

Travis starts laughing moronically. I glance over at him, arching my eyebrows.

"She's already kicking you out, bro, and you haven't even started the honeymoon phase...Whatever you're doing, you're doing it wrong."

I smile at Travis. Honestly, he is the biggest idiot of all time. Doesn't he know he shouldn't insult his alpha?

"Don't worry. I'll give you the pointers. I'm a love master."

"Is that why Lisa is still upstairs?"

Lucas chuckles softly as Travis's mouth drops open as he tries to come up with an answer. He then glares and stands.

"Lisa!" he yells, storming towards the staircase. "Tell them I am a love master!" he shouts at the bottom of the stairs.

The only response we get is a hysterical laugh from up in my bedroom. I smile, placing a hand over my mouth to keep from laughing as well. Lisa just shot Travis down, and it is by far the most entertaining scene in my life.

Travis runs up the stairs, leaving Lucas and me.

It's going to be hard to be away from you, Lucas says, wrapping an arm around my waist.

I sigh, sitting on his lap to wrap my arms around his neck. "I know. But we can do it."

Is breá liom tú, mac tíre beag. (I love you, little wolf.)

I smile and place a deep kiss on his lips. "As I love you, *mo alfa* (my alpha)."

Thirteen

Mae

October 11, 2036

"You never told me it was this intense," I say to my mom as she hands me another towel-wrapped ice pack.

I open it to see that she put the ice in a ziplock bag. Discarding the towel, I place the bag of ice directly on my forehead, letting out a shivering sigh.

After a brutal night of sweating bullets and yearning for Lucas's touch, I decided that I needed to distance myself. Whenever I am around him, I am so tempted to touch him. When I am not with him, I am plotting ways to take him down.

"It's only this bad because you didn't complete the mating bond," Lisa says from the kitchen stool beside me.

Lucas has ensured that I travel with someone, too concerned that I won't be able to make it to the Shadow pack safely. I understand completely, considering the revenge-seeking mass of rogues out there. Lisa has volunteered. At first, I refused, not wanting to keep her from her mate, but she insisted.

"How can you have a mate that looks like that and still be a virgin?" Aunt Natalie asks, stepping up behind me. She gathers my hair in her hands and twists it into a high bun.

A second later, another bag of ice is placed on the back on my neck. I let out a coo, allowing the coolness relieve me.

I smile like an idiot. She is right, but if I had a choice, I would have mated with Lucas many days ago. But I respect him wanting to wait.

"Honestly, I have no idea how I have the strength. Especially when he steps out of the shower in the mornings…The water droplets on his sculpted chest…" I feel my body start aflame, causing the ice to melt.

"Oh my…" Aunt Natalie breathes as she steps back and fans her face.

I burst out laughing along with Lisa and my mother.

"If you don't mate with that young man, I will."

I know she is kidding. She will never look at another man, not when she has Trent who is most definitely the love of her life.

Uncle Trent walks into the kitchen, slapping Aunt Natalie's butt. "You will what?" Trent growls, and Natalie giggles, turning to look up at him.

"You're so old. I need a newer, improved version of yourself."

Lisa chokes on her milk beside me as my aunt says this. I drop my head into my hands, embarrassed. I am just glad it isn't Lucas who is here.

"*Tá tú teaghlach suimiúil.* (You have an interesting family)," Lisa whispers over to me.

"*Tá mé chomh leithscéal.* (I'm so sorry.)" I shake my head.

Even though I know what it is I want to say, I totally butchered the accent and the fluency. It is going to take a lot of work to be able to articulate the language correctly.

"You speak Gaelic now?" I hear my mom ask. She leans against the kitchen counter, looking at me with a confused expression.

"Erm, yeah. The Cipher pack speaks Gaelic…It's to ensure pack secrets," I tell her.

My mom gives Trent and Natalie a look before she offers me a soft smile and leaves the kitchen. I watch her retreating form until she is out of sight. Then I turn to my aunt and uncle, raising my eyebrow.

"You're growing up, kiddo. And moving on. It's hard on her," Trent says, wrapping an arm around Natalie's waist, placing a kiss on her temple.

"*Agus shíl mé Travis agus bhí mé dona.* (And I thought Travis and I were bad.)"

I just shake my head at Lisa's statement. She was speaking to herself, so I didn't respond. Even though I agree wholeheartedly.

"Hey!"

I hear an obnoxious shout from the back door. I look to see Blondie walk into the house, pointing to me.

"I know you!" he proclaims.

I smile like an idiot and push off the stool to run over and jump into Uncle Mason's arms. He squishes me tight against his chest, letting out a grunt.

"I've missed you, squirt."

I grin up at him, shrugging my shoulders as I reach up and pat his face. "Yeah, well, why wouldn't you?" I ask.

Mason squints down at me, his lips dipping down into a small frown. I watch as his eyes begin to water, tears threatening to fall out.

My stomach twists—"I missed you too, Mason"— and I thump his chest.

His lips turn into a wide grin, and he brushes his fake tears away. "Knew it." Then he turns to Lisa. "Hello, I'm Mason, this geek's uncle." Mason motions to me as he offers Lisa a handshake.

"It's nice to meet you…I can see where she gets her geekiness from," Lisa remarks.

Mason laughs, nodding. "That's good."

"Where's my dad?" I ask.

Mason frowns again and crosses his arms over his chest. "He's dealing with the Prowler pack."

That is something I don't understand. The Prowler pack has always been a good ally to us, after the Castor incident. What has prompted them to suddenly turn on us? Jenny will never do that to my mother. They are best friends.

"What's going on, Mason?"

"They're harboring rogues."

I snarl. That is against the werewolf law. You are not allowed to give shelter to the disloyal wolves who abandon their packs. I want to go and make that abundantly clear.

"We don't know why. But they quit doing patrols, and they never make appearances for the monthly report. Landon was getting frustrated. He went to speak with Alpha Tyler. Jenny finally admitted to the rogues. Now Landon and Alpha Marcus are speaking with Tyler and Jenny."

Marcus is the Alpha of the Rose pack. He has always been faithful to my dad. He won't betray us.

"I'm going." I step away from Mason and exit the house before he can even think of stopping me. I sprint towards the gathering area where the discussions always take place with the three packs.

It is placed deep into the forest, in the center of all three packs. There is a large opening where all of us can fit if we have a meeting.

When I arrive, the three men are speaking with so much anger that my hair bristles at the back of my neck. I march over to where they are standing, and when I reach Tyler, I shove him hard on the chest, not liking how close he is to my father. Tyler snarls at me, glaring.

"Mae! What are you doing here?" My father grabs my arm, pulling me back so I am behind him. "Go home."

"Why would you be harboring rogues?" I snap over at Tyler.

He arches his eyebrow at me, crossing his arms across his chest. "Watch your tone, girl."

"We are equals, Tyler. I don't bow to you."

His eyes narrow into slits as he stares at me. Tyler was never intimidating. He was always the sweetest guy, acting as another uncle towards me. I have never thought that he can act so coldly towards me.

"Mae, please go home." My father begs.

"Tell me." I demand, crossing my arms as well to signify I am not leaving until I get what I am looking for.

"Who said we are harboring rogues, Mae?" Tyler asks, arching an eyebrow.

I glance over my shoulder to see my father pleading me with his eyes. What is he trying to hide from me?

"Well, you are, aren't you? It doesn't matter who says it."

Tyler scoffs, shaking his head. "We're not giving shelter to rogues. We're imprisoning them."

I am taken back by what he is saying. Imprisoning them? Why is he be doing that?

"Why?"

"You stupid girl. Why do you think? The Cipher pack has been targeted. Every rogue is turning their attention towards you. I don't know why, but you are now deemed a threat to them, and they wish to annihilate you."

"Me? What did I do?" I ask, looking over at my father.

He shakes his head, his eyes soft as tears gather in them. He's scared. I have never seen my father scared, but here, standing before me, my father is frightened. It is chilling. When we're young, girls think of their fathers as their heroes, invincible and never cowering from any opposing force. Yet here I stand to see my dad is just as vulnerable as the next person.

I walk over and grab one of his hands. "It's okay. I'll be okay." I offer him a smile, trying to convince the both of us.

"We're capturing rogues to figure out what they know. Then we kill them."

I look over at Tyler, trying to summon the disgust that I know I should be feeling. But all I feel is gratitude.

"Which is wrong!" My father snarls.

Yes, that is what my father always taught me: never kill a defenseless man.

"Each rogue we kill is one less rogue trying to tear your daughter apart!"

I wince at his words. He's trying to get through my father's thick skull, and the only way to do so is to be brutally honest.

I let out a deep sigh as they go back to bickering. All I can think about is how Lucas is at the pack, where he can be attacked at any moment. I need to get back. If we are to be attacked as Tyler has said, then we will be together when that happens.

Fourteen

Mae

October 11, 2036

Lisa and I hurry back to the Cipher pack. Having explained the danger to Lisa, she is just as determined to leave as I am. The heat is now forgotten, though I know it will return when I see Lucas.

I have to be the one to warn him. I have to be with him.

The drive home is quicker than usual, for I am going twenty over the speed limit. Lisa is a bit nervous about my driving, but half the time, I am blocking her out.

The moment we pull up in the driveway, Travis stepped out of the house, looking confused. Yes, we were literally at the Shadow pack for two hours before we turned around and came back here.

I throw the car in park, pull the key from the ignition, and hop out to jog towards Travis.

"He's okay?" I ask.

Travis nods slowly, his eyes portraying the fact that he thinks I am a crazy person.

Maybe I am.

I walk briskly through the front lawn and head for Lucas's office. Pushing open the big oak doors, I see him sitting at the desk, writing something down. Upon hearing the door open, he peeks up as if expecting Travis. When he notices it's me, his eyes darken, and his spine straightens.

My wolf screams for me to tear off all his clothes and complete the bond. Here. Now.

But I am able to push her back as I walk slowly towards him, each step making it harder to resist. I swear, if he even flicks his beautiful hair out of his eyes, it will be my undoing. He just needs to sit there like a statue.

"We need to talk," I grumble, sitting at the chair across his desk.

Lucas leans forward, placing his elbows on the desk and his hands clasped together in front of him.

"I just spoke with Alpha Tyler of the Prowler pack. He has imprisoned rogues and is killing them."

Why? Why would he do that?

"He has been informed that the rogues have targeted the Cipher pack." I decide to leave the part where they are more specifically targeting me. All I care about at this moment is ensuring the pack's safety, along with Lucas's.

This is outrageous. I grant them their freedom, and they now turn every rogue against me. What have I done to elicit such an act? Lucas runs his hands through his hair.

I want to tell him that it isn't anything he had done, that all of this is somehow my fault, but I don't understand as well.

What did I do to make every rogue want me dead?

"It's going to be alright, Lucas. We have the Rose, Prowler, and Shadow pack. It will be alright," I say, trying to convince the both of us.

Lucas sighs before he tilts his head up to look at me. *I never wanted this kind of life for you. I wanted you to live a life full of happiness and peace and love.*

I reach over and grab his left hand, giving it a squeeze.

People are going to die. People we love.

As he says this, my stomach clenches as a tear rolls down my cheek. He's right. We're going to lose those closest to us. This will be a battle that will be told through many generations. It will go down in history.

I bite my bottom lip and lean back in my chair, wiping my tear away. "Was it a child's dream to think we'd actually have a family?"

Lucas's big brown eyes stare into my own, a frown on his lips. He just looks at me.

I'm jumping to conclusions, assuming that one of us or both of us won't make it out alive. It's unwise, but I can't help but sense the impending doom that is looming over us.

I just wish we had more time.

We will have a family, Mae. I won't let our story end here. Lucas gets to his feet and walks over to grab my hand, pulling me from my seat.

I gaze up at him as he wraps an arm around my waist and leans down to press a hot kiss to my lips. I moan, reaching up to sink my fingers into his hair as he grips tight to my hips. I jump up as he easily hoists me so my legs wind around his waist.

Lucas places his hands under my butt to hold me up as I lean back and peel off my shirt. His eyes zero into my bra-clad breasts, and he growls softly.

We can't complete the bond in my office...

"Yes, we can." I smash my lips to his again, quieting him from any doubts.

I bite his bottom lip as he lowers us to the large rug, his hands trailing down my bare sides softly until they reach my shorts. His finger hook under the band, and in a swift movement, he rips them off and tosses them with my shirt. Lucas then gathers his shirt and discards it before he falls back to capture my mouth with his.

My heart races as I run my nails up and down his smooth tanned back.

This is actually happening.

Lucas trails kisses down my neck, along my collarbone and down to my breasts. My breathing hitches as he rises and leans back to admire me underneath him.

You're so beautiful.

I blush like an idiot, wanting to hide my embarrassment. "I love you, Lucas Donovan. Make me yours."

And he did. We made love in his office for hours. We only stopped when exhaustion overcame us, causing us to fall asleep in each other's arms on the floor.

* * *

When I wake up, I groan at the pain in my hip. Sleeping on the floor certainly isn't good for the bones. Lucas's arm is draped over my waist, his chest pressed against my back. His steady breathing tells me that he is asleep.

A smirk stretches across my face as I remember the events of last night. I don't think we will ever be fully sated. We had quite a few rounds, and I am sure we would have kept going if we weren't so drained from the heat, the news on the rogues, and the cardio we were doing.

I blush, knowing very well that Travis, Lisa, and everyone else would have heard us. The office isn't exactly soundproof, and we weren't particularly quiet.

Travis is going to give me an earful.

Lucas's arm tightens as he pulls me closer to his chest, groaning.

Stop thinking, he grumbles beside me.

I look over my shoulder to see his eyes squeezed tight as he tries to go back to sleep. "I can't. I am blissfully happy." I roll, so I am facing him, placing a kiss to his pouting lips.

Lucas grins and gives me a kiss back. *Well, what can I say? I know how to please the ladies...*

"Okay, Travis." I roll my eyes, causing Lucas to chuckle as he squeezes me close one last time.

Time to get back to reality.

I groan and push Lucas so he is lying on his back and my head is resting on his chest.

"But I love this fantasy...This dreamland...Now I definitely wish we had more time," I say.

Lucas places a kiss on the top of my head, sighing softly. *I know, little wolf. But I promise we will be doing much more of this...We'll have to with the twelve kids we're going to have.*

I burst out laughing in hysteria at his pipe dream. That is never going to happen.

Getting to my feet, I get dressed in my discarded clothes. I gaze down at myself and instantly feel self-conscious about walking out of the office. Everyone will know what transpired last night and I try to brace myself for the witty comments.

I head for the door, but Lucas grabs my hand, halting me.

Wait. I have something to tell you.

I arch my eyebrows. Whenever someone says that after sex, it's usually followed by "I have herpes" or "the condom broke..." Not exactly the phrase one wants to hear.

Tá sé agat an moan teo. (You've got the hottest moan.)

I slap Lucas's arm before I spin on my heel and storm out of the office, heading to the kitchen where Travis, Lisa, and Jake are eating a variety of breakfast options. Lisa has a knowing smirk on her face. Jake is picking at his waffle, and Travis has an evil grin.

"Good morning, Moaning Mae."

My eyes narrow into slits as I growl at him, yanking open the fridge.

"Did you sleep well?" he asks, his voice an octave higher than usual, testing my patience. He is asking for me to slap him.

"I slept perfectly"—I grab orange juice and pour it into a plastic cup—"and you? Did you sleep well?" I take a sip as I stare down my glass at him.

"Heavens no. There was too much moaning."

I don't think twice as I chuck my half-filled cup of orange juice at him. Travis throws his hands up to shield his face as the cup hits his side and clatters on the floor, successfully getting him wet.

Travis doesn't mind. He just laughs as if he were the funniest man on Earth.

Lucas enters the kitchen, wrapping his arm around me from behind, placing a kiss at the nape of my neck.

"Well, if it isn't Lusty Luc?" Travis says.

He's asking for his death at this point.

Lucas glares at him from over my shoulder, shaking his head. Then he shoots him a threat in Gaelic. However, it's too fast for me to understand. Travis has a look of horror at whatever Lucas said. He goes back to eating his bacon and eggs. I shake my head and lean back against Lucas, loving being in his arms.

"I love you," I whisper in his ear.

Lucas kisses up my neck and takes my earlobe between his teeth gently. *I love you more.*

Of course, that isn't possible, but I don't voice my opinion. I am just happy to be in such a sated, peaceful state that even the discussion of the rogues can't ruin it.

Alas, Lucas brings it up. Jake and Travis already knew. Lisa told them while I was preoccupied.

"You're sure your father's packs will fight with us?" Travis asks.

I lean forward, resting my elbows on the kitchen counter and placing my chin in the palm of my hand. Lucas draws lazy circles on my back.

"Of course. I'm sure many packs will stand with us against the rogues." I look over my shoulder at Lucas. "We can contact the Downer pack and the Coast pack. You've mentioned they're reliable allies, right?"

Yes. We will enlist our friends' help. He reaches down and trails his fingers over my cheek. *We will send out a distress call to packs all over the country. As you've said, many packs will stand against the rogues.*

I nod, smiling softly that he's listening to my advice and carrying it out. Alphas are usually stubborn and wish to manifest the ideas on their own.

"Good. Lisa, Travis, will you inform the rest of the pack? Jake, Lucas, and I will travel to the neighboring packs and speak to them." I stand up straight and clap my hands, sealing my plan and causing everyone to jump into action.

Travis and Lisa exit quickly, and Jake turns to look at us, a frown on his face. Lucas touches my face gently in his hands, his thumbs running across my cheekbones.

I promise you, Mae, we will have many more days like this. Lucas seals his promise with a kiss.

Fifteen

Mae

October 12, 2036

After Jake, Luc, and I visit the neighboring packs, we weren't surprised that they both agreed to join forces with us. All packs are strongly against the retaliation of rogues. They disobey the Werewolf Law, therefore they are outcasts. However, for them to think they can target one pack and not have others join in the fight, they are sorely mistaken.

Lisa and Travis had the job of informing the rest of the pack, so when we got back home, everyone was already rallied together. Lucas is about to go up and speak to the pack, but I place a hand on his chest to stop him. I instead walk up to take his place.

I clear my throat, wringing my fingers together as nerves settle in the pit of my stomach. My father has taught me all I need to know when addressing a pack. I was never nervous when I spoke to the Shadow pack. But this is different. This is my pack, my responsibility.

"As you are all aware, there has been word of an attack towards our pack. We do not know why the rogues are targeting us, but I want you all to be aware that this fight is most definitely in our favor." My eyes scan the crowd until they land on Elizabeth, the elder, who is walking through the crowd, her eyes glaring at me as she makes her way to the forest.

I know I should stop her, but at this moment, all I want is for her lying, scheming self to get the hell out of my pack.

"Currently, we have recruited a number of packs, and as the days go on, more will join our cause. My uncle will continue to talk to the rogues until we get an idea when they will attack. Until then, be diligent and keep your eyes open. We will double patrol to ensure that no one gets in or out of this territory without Lucas's or my permission. I hate to put this pack on lockdown. You don't deserve this; however, I am only thinking of your safety." I take a deep breath and look over my shoulder to see Lucas standing with his arms crossed over his chest. He arches an eyebrow at me and offers a charming smirk. "Alright. You're dismissed. Report to your gamma to find out your patrol shift."

I turn and walk towards Lucas, sliding into his arms as he wraps them around my shoulders, pulling me close to his chest. I slip my arms around his waist and gather the back of his shirt into my fists, clinging onto him.

Your father taught you well. You're a natural alpha.

"So are you," I whisper, pulling back to smile up at him. "We should head inside. Speak with my father and see what they found out."

* * *

"All the rogue is telling them is that it's already in action," I tell Lucas, Lisa, Travis, and Jake.

They stare at me with looks of shock and anxiety.

So, when exactly are they going to strike? How long have they been "in action?" I don't know. They could be a day away or a week.

My father has already uprooted his pack warriors and are traveling to set camp in our territory. The Rose pack will camp out in the Coast pack's territory, and the Prowler pack will be with the Downer pack.

Lucas has sent word to all the packs throughout the country, asking for their aid. We haven't heard back from any of them, which concerns me. There could be tens of thousands of rogues. If they have assembled from all over the world, just imagine how many that could be, considering we have a few hundred packs in the United States alone. Every pack has members that are disloyal, that have to be cast away.

I shake my head, scratching behind my ear as I grow nervous. I glance at Lucas who is rubbing his eyebrows as if trying to rid himself of stress.

It's going to be alright, mo ghrá. We'll get through this. We'll be ready for them.

I nod. He's right. We know they're on their way. We have five packs fighting with us. We can survive this.

We have to.

Lucas has to survive this.

I lean against the desk in Lucas's office and dismiss Lisa, Jake, and Travis. They leave without another word, and Lucas walks over to place his hands on my hips. I tilt my head back to look up at him.

"Guess what," I whisper, reaching up to run my fingers through his short beard.

He hasn't shaved in two days, and it's nearly a full beard that would take some men weeks to grow. Lucas looks good with a beard. He looks older, wiser, and sexier.

What? he asks, resting his forehead against mine.

"I love you."

Lucas smiles and places a hard kiss to my lips, sending chills throughout my body. I wonder if there will ever be a day when his kiss doesn't affect me in such a way. Or will I always grow weak just by his touch?

I love you more.

I roll my eyes and slide my hand back so it's buried in his thick hair. I grip tightly, keeping him close as I kiss him again. Lucas growls and lifts me so I am sitting on his desk with him in between my legs.

My hands gently move down his back to the hem of his shirt where I slide my hands underneath, my nails scraping against his soft skin. Lucas pulls back to place a kiss on my neck, claiming my mark and sucking hard. I hiss and push him away the same time I am holding him closer. My body screams with fire and passion as I drop my head against his shoulder, afflicting the same torture to him.

Lucas grabs my shorts and start to pull them off. Before he can even unbutton it, there is a loud scream that sounds throughout the house. I freeze, my blood running cold. Lucas steps back, his eyes bewildered as we bolt towards the door in a hurry. I struggle to keep up with him as he hightails it to the backyard, where I take in the sight before me.

I gasp, coming to a stop to see Travis's wolf fighting with another. People are gathering, watching with wide eyes as the two wolves look as if they are on the verge of killing each other. Stepping away from Lucas, I run to grab the wolf on top of Travis and shove him off, growling lowly.

"Shift." I order.

The man does as he's told, looking up at me with angry eyes as he rips a pair of basketball shorts out of a woman's offering hand. Micah pulls them on and stands, crossing his arms over his chest. My eyes run over him, taking in every feature. His hair is jet black with eyes that match. His cheekbones are angular and sharp as he glares, his jaw ticking as if he's keeping a choice of words within. He has angry scars adorning his chest that seem relatively fresh. He doesn't look familiar, but that doesn't surprise me. I am still relatively new; I have not met everyone in the pack.

"What is the meaning of this?" I snarl. "Who started it?" I ask, crossing my arms.

Travis sits, squinting his eyes over to the other wolf. *He did*, Travis says, his voice gruff with anger and annoyance.

"What is your name?" I look over at the wolf who by now has transformed into his human form.

"Micah," the man answers.

I look Micah up and down, frowning. I've never heard of a wolf named Micah and the fact that he doesn't look even remotely familiar.

Before I could think through what I was doing, I reach forward and slide my fingers through his hair. They close around the strands, and I use my grip to yank his head forward and down, meeting my knee. His nose crunches under the impact, and I use his vulnerability to shove him to his knees.

"Where are they?" I snarl.

What are you doing? Lucas yells through our mind link.

I ignore him and loom over Micah.

"Answer me. Where are they?"

"What are you going on about?" Micah asks, not sounding the least bit confused.

Mae?

"He's a rogue, Lucas. Do you know of anyone named Micah in this pack?"

When Lucas doesn't respond, I return my attention back to Micah. I grab his throat and squeeze tight, glaring at him. He doesn't struggle, not even when blood trails down to his collarbone from my nails digging into his skin.

"When will they be here?" I bite out.

Micah only smiles at me, only fueling my anger. I throw him to the ground by the neck and grab his hair again, lifting his head to gain momentum before slamming it to the ground.

Mae, enough! Lucas snaps.

I push him out of my head as I continue to beat the man underneath me. He is going to answer me, even if it's the last thing he says.

Pausing for a moment to check to see if he will answer, all I get is a strangled chuckle. Growling, I raise my fist up to deliver a blow. However, arms grab my sides and lift me off the ground.

"Mae, stop." His deep voice shakes through me.

My father.

I shake my dad's hands off me and look to see Lucas staring at me with a look of sadness. I know I disappointed him and my father. I shouldn't have lost my control like that.

"Where are they?" I ask again, this time with a calmer voice.

Micah lies on the ground, staring up at the sky as he lets out a sigh. A bloody smile takes its place on his face as he turns to look at me.

"They're already here."

Sixteen

Mae

October 12, 2036

"Where is Lucas?" I scream on the top of my lungs as I storm through the house, watching all the members of my pack step aside to make way for me.

Most of the members are lying on the floor, clutching some part of their anatomy that is wounded, groaning in pain. The others are attending to the wounded.

Apparently, our house has become a hospital.

I continue to search through all the hallways, searching for Lucas among the wounded. I know he got hurt. I saw him. I saw the fatal blow to the chest, the bite to the neck. I have to find him. Now.

"Lucas!" I yell, ignoring the people who told me to keep it down.

"Mae!"

I spin to see Lisa standing in front of me, covered in blood. My eyes widen as I run over to examine her.

"It-it's not mine." She stutters, shaking as she holds her arms out.

"Whose?" I whisper.

Her bottom lip trembles as she shakes her head, looking into my eyes. "I'm so sorry."

Pulling my eyebrows together, I tilt my head slightly, my eyes unfocused as I realize what she is saying.

"We-we did ev-everything we co-could," Lisa says, choking out sobs.

"Where is he?" I mutter.

"Office."

I break out into a run, sprinting to the office where I throw open the big oak doors and stop cold at the sight in front of me.

I gasp, sucking in a breath as I feel like caving into myself. Raising a hand to cover my mouth, I let out a shaky sob.

Travis is kneeling on the floor, pounding his fist against Lucas's chest repeatedly. I watch my mate lying still, only jolting at the impact of Travis's fist. Blood coats Lucas's body, which keeps oozing at the cuts on his chest and the bite marks on his neck. I stumble over to Travis, dropping down beside him to hover over Lucas.

"Oh no. No, no, no. This isn't possible." I reach up and place soft hands on Lucas's stone cold face.

He doesn't move. No sparks are ignited with the touch. It's just empty, dead.

"This isn't possible. This isn't real. This is just a nightmare. It's just a nightmare. You're not dead. You're not dead!" Tears roll down my cheeks as I reach up and throw my hair into a quick bun, looking over at Travis. "You have to save him. How do we save him?" I ask as he continues to pound on Lucas's chest, trying to start his heart.

Travis doesn't answer me, only continuing his attempt to revive him. Lisa walks in and stands behind me, shaking in shock.

"Travis, what do I do?"

No answer. I begin to panic, the reality sinking in. I've lost my mate.

"What do I do?" I cry, bending down to cling to Lucas's cold body, sobbing into his shoulder.

This can't be happening. This is only a nightmare.

Lucas isn't dead.

He can't be.

* * *

ONE HOUR EARLIER

"They're already here."

I spin around and look at Lucas with wide eyes. He storms forward and grabs onto my arm, looking me dead in the eyes.

You do not leave my side. Do you understand, mo ghrá?

I nod quickly, watching as everything happens so fast.

Within moments, all the wolves are rallied, forming behind the six alphas and six lunas. I look over to my mom and dad, praying this isn't the last time I see them. My father gives me a nod before he shifts into his wolf.

Turning again to Lucas, I reach up to give him a short but hot kiss. He gives one back, gripping my hair tightly.

Stay alive, he says, following my father's actions by taking upon his dark grey wolf.

I follow suit, standing beside him as my hair bristles at my neck.

Let this be quick and painless.

Rogues emerge from the trees, advancing from all sides. Fighting in our backyard is tight. Even though our yard is very large with two acres to work with, it is claustrophobic with all the wolves crowding it.

Rogues, most of them being away from packs for so long, have forgotten the training alphas enforce. Some are weak; however, others are very powerful. I notice a wolf fighting Lucas to my right, one who held his own against an alpha. It is surprising; however, it shows just how much the rogues have evolved.

I lose count of how many rogues I killed. I just tear through them, not thinking of anything but getting to the end of this battle.

When a wolf comes to my left and blindsides me, I am thrown to the ground in a grunt. I look up to see him pounce on top of me. Growling, I struggle beneath him. I have never been good at fighting from below. It is in my genes to be the one who is on top, who is demanding authority. I don't submit, especially to rogues.

Upon hearing a cry, I whip my head around to see Lucas collapse to the ground, blood coating the white patch of fur on his chest.

The black rogue lunges down, sinking his teeth into his neck. Snarling, I shove the rogue off me, twist to my feet, and run to aid my mate. I leap forward, colliding with the black wolf, causing us to roll away from Lucas.

Once we stop rolling, I pin him down beneath me and snarl in his face, saliva dripping from my blood-stained teeth as I glare down at him. No one hurts my mate. Without another thought, I snake forward and take the rogue's face in between my jaws. Once my teeth make contact with his skull, I bite hard until the bone is crushed.

Stepping back, I look up to see retreating wolves. Well, that was most definitely quick. I can't say it was painless, however.

Shifting back to my human form, I search for Lucas, stepping around the dead warriors, looking for my mate. However, I see people already being lifted from the field and taken to both the infirmary and the pack house.

"Lucas!" I yell, spinning in a circle to see if anyone reacted to my call.

Lucas! I shout, trying him through the mind link, but I come up with nothing.

I see my father crouched down beside a wounded warrior, and I run over only to gasp and let out a scream, doubling over as this unbearable pain settles in my stomach.

"Mason!" I drop down, searching for any signs of life.

My dad looks up at me with tears in his eyes, shaking his head.

"No!" I grip my hair, pulling gently as I begin to hyperventilate.

"Where is Lucas?" my father asks, and I shake my head, looking around the battlefield again. "You need to find him. Mae! Go find him."

I push up to my feet and take a step back, shaking my head again. "Dad…"

"Mae. Check the house. Go, sweetie."

Landon Matthews doesn't want me to see Mason Danielson, his best friend, lying on a bloody field. Landon Matthews doesn't want me to see him cry. Biting my bottom lip, I run into the house, trying to compose myself in order to find Lucas.

Once I step into the house, I shout, "Where is Lucas?"

* * *

I hug my knees to my chest as I sit beside Lucas's corpse, tears rolling down my cheeks as I stare at him, willing him to wake up, to come back to me.

How can he be dead? How can the Moon Goddess set us up, only to be together for a short amount of time? What kind of cruelty is this? To have a mere kiss of a life I could have with Lucas.

I hang my head, resting my forehead against my knees as a sob shakes through me, a hysterical scream escaping my lips.

The office door is pushed open, and I look to see my mother walk in, a frown on her face as tears trail down her cheeks as well. My eyes widen and I jump up to my feet, running over to grab onto her arm. She nearly collapses into me, embracing me into a hug.

"Natalie."

My knees buckle and together we fall to the ground. I let out another scream, gripping tightly to my mom as if she is the only thing that can keep me from losing myself. I feel as if my very heart is being taken from my chest. Natalie and Mason. The two people I looked up to, idolized. They were a second mother and father to me. They were more than an aunt and uncle. They were my best friends.

And Lucas. My sweet, young Lucas who doesn't deserve this in the least. He barely had the chance to live. He didn't get to see his son's birth and to watch him grow into a handsome man and find love. He didn't get the chance to regain his voice, to finally become whole again. Instead, he died, his life unfulfilled.

Dad…Oh my goddess. He just lost two very important people…His sister. I get to my feet, helping my mom up before I run through the house, searching for my father. I find him in the backyard, sitting beside the lifeless bodies of Mason and Natalie. He is staring at them, tears rolling endlessly down his cheeks. Seeing my father cry brings an unknown emotion to the surface, making me walk over and sit beside him. Landon rests his head against my shoulder as we both cry together.

"I am so sorry for you loss, sweetie." His voice is hoarse, dry from the crying.

I stare at Natalie, her dark hair fanned out and her usual rosy cheeks now pale. Her lips that always held a smile are now pressed into a firm line, never to curve upward again. I will miss her smile. I will miss her laugh and Mason's lame jokes and pet names. I will miss Lucas's touch and his warm embrace. I will miss feeling whole.

"This has to be a nightmare," I whisper.

"I want nothing more than for that to be so, sweetheart. But we both know this is cold reality."

I hear movement, and I lift my eyes to see Trent sit beside Natalie's head. His eyes are bloodshot as he looks at me, holding nothing but pure depression on his features. He's dead inside, just as I am.

"Where is Jesse?" I ask, nodding to Mason.

"Infirmary. She will be okay, but she doesn't know," my dad says, staring off into the distance as he says this.

Jesse doesn't know that Mason is dead. She doesn't know that she will never get kissed by him again or laugh at his goofiness.

No. No more Mason.

No more Natalie.

No more Lucas.

I bite my bottom lip to keep another wave of tears from coming.

"Mae."

I look up to see Jenny. I jump to my feet and run into her arms, holding on tightly.

"You're okay," she whispers, and I nod, pulling back to wipe my tears away. "Lucas?" I shake my head, my lip quivering.

"Tyler?"

Jenny reluctantly nods, reaching over to run her fingers through my hair.

"It's going to be okay, Mae. You're going to be okay." She looks down at Mason and Natalie, letting out a shaky breath. "Life will be much different now, but you will be okay."

"Yes. Yes, you're right. I will be alright." I nod. I have to be.

The Cipher pack is now mine. I have to be strong for them, no matter the pain I will feel every day, no matter how much I want to give up. I have to be the leader they deserve.

I pull away. "It's time to say goodbye." I kneel on the ground and stare at Mason. "I would never admit it to you, but I actually really loved it when you called me squirt. I really wish I had told you that. I am going to miss you so much, Uncle Mason. You will always be in my heart." I place a kiss to his cheek before I turn to Natalie. "This wasn't how you were supposed to die, Natalie. You were supposed to leave this world dressed in a beautiful, obnoxious dress, lying in bed with your hair perfectly combed. You were supposed to pass just as a princess would. I am going to miss you as well." I give her a kiss on the cheek as well.

Rubbing my hands, I get to my feet and reluctantly make my way back to the office where I will say goodbye to Lucas and where I will see him for the last time.

I sit beside his lifeless form and grab his hand, holding it in my own. "You told me we would have a family. That our story wouldn't end with this battle. But you lied. Our story ends right here. It's okay, Luc. I forgive you. I'm just sorry that I couldn't give you what you wanted, what you needed, and what you deserved. You deserved so much better than what was laid out for you, and I am so sorry." I lift his hand up and press a kiss to his palm. "I don't want to say goodbye. I don't want to finalize this. I am not ready to live in a life without you." I look over at his face and frown.

I notice something peculiar. Something that shouldn't have happened. His throat is healed. Coming to alert, I examine his chest, brushing away the dried blood to find scars in place of the cuts. My eyes flicker up to his face again to see his lips parted.

A small yet noticeable raise of his chest is felt under my hand.

Impossible.

Lucas lets out a breath. "Mae."

Seventeen

Mae

October 14, 2036

It's been two days since Lucas awoke, speaking my name. Now, he lies in bed, not moving, barely breathing. He is force fed soup to give him sustenance, to keep him alive.

Mason and Natalie were buried yesterday at noon. Jesse was able to say goodbye to Mason, and when the funeral was over, the Rose, Shadow, and Prowler pack went back to their territories. Jesse didn't say goodbye to me; she blames me for Mason's death. My mother told me to give her some time, but I know she is right.

The rogues that Tyler tortured said they targeted the Cipher pack because of me. Mason and Natalie wouldn't be dead if it wasn't for me and whatever the reason the rogues had to plan an attack.

There is only one person I know who has all the answers I want and need: Elizabeth. I knew it was a mistake to just watch her leave. I should have captured her. She would have been at our disposal for questioning.

My father couldn't look at me when he left. Was it because he blames me as well or because he doesn't want me to see his vulnerability? I am not sure. However, the feeling I experienced was devastating. I am a "daddy's girl," and I thought we were closer than that.

I curl into a ball, my head resting on the pillow beside Lucas. My eyes focus on him, refusing to gaze somewhere else in case he wakes up or makes any movement. His heartbeat is steady, strong. I know he will be okay. However, I don't know how long it will be until he awakens for good.

Grabbing his right hand with both of mine, I clutch it to my chest and let out a deep sigh. My father will scold me for being weak, for lying in bed while my pack needs reassurance, a plan, or anything to keep them going. But how can I speak to them about hope, about a better future when I am looking at my own and not knowing if it, in fact, will be good. I can't promise them anything even though that is what they need. I can't tell them everything will be alright because this isn't over.

"I wish you could just open your eyes," I whisper, reaching up and tucking a piece of blond hair away from his forehead. "*Is breá liom tú, mo maité. Tar ar ais chugam.* (I love you, my mate. Come back to me.)"

*   *   *

On the fourth day of Lucas lying in a coma, I head downstairs to see Travis and Lisa. I appoint Travis in command while I am otherwise unavailable. However, I come to realize that Lucas won't want me lying in bed beside him, waiting for his eyes to open. He will want me to make sure the pack is functioning, that everyone else is alright before caring for him.

And quite frankly, I don't feel well lying all day, not being productive. I need to be out and about, helping this pack recover. It will help time pass quicker, and Lucas will wake up eventually.

Lisa is sitting at the breakfast bar, eating a stack on pancakes as I take a seat next to her. Her eyes travel from her plate to my elbows on the counter and follow my arms up to my face. She has a look of awe and shock adorning her features.

"You're here," she whispers, mostly to herself.

I smile. "Yeah, I'm here, and I'm starving." I reach over the counter and pull the silverware drawer open to grab a fork.

I don't ask permission, and I just stab a pancake and tear a piece off, shoving it in my mouth. Lisa doesn't react, only watching me as if I am a ghost.

"These are delicious pancakes," I say, trying to break her from her trance.

"Natalie and Mason are dead."

Just like that, all the pain and dread I managed to push aside resurfaces. I place my fork on the counter and turn to face Lisa.

"I know."

"Lucas is in a coma."

"I know."

"Half of the pack is still in the infirmary."

"Lisa, I know."

"Then what are you doing—"

"I'm trying to make light of the situation. I am trying to forget, just for a moment, that everything has gone to crap and just eat a pancake with my best friend." I growl, turning back and gathering another piece of pancake on my fork.

I angrily eat, my anger causing the food to taste bland.

"I didn't lose anyone, Mae. I don't know what you're going through, but I think you have ignored their death for too long."

"I said my goodbyes. It's done."

Lisa frowns over at me. "You said goodbye, but you're not accepting it. You're pushing your feelings aside, but you need to come to terms with the fact that they're gone and allow yourself to grieve."

I bite my bottom lip, staring intently on the stove and microwave, trying to keep my eyes dry.

Why is she doing this?

"Natalie will never play with your hair again."

I grip the fork in my hand tightly, feeling the cool metal bending under my force. She's doing this on purpose. She wants me to be angry.

"Mason will never call you 'squirt' again."

I push away from the counter and snarl at her, my hands forming into fists at my side.

"Why are you doing this?"

"Because you need to feel something for their loss, be it anger or sadness. It has to be something so you can move on. If not, you'll be stuck in limbo, never letting go!" Lisa says, getting to her feet as well so we're standing face to face.

"Well, I'm angry."

"At who?"

"The—the rogues. The rogues who killed them," I say, shaking my head.

Lisa crosses her arms. "Yes, but you don't know who they are. You can't be mad at someone you don't know. So who are you really mad at?"

I glare at her. I'm really mad at the rogues who killed my family. I'm mad at all of them. I want every last one of them to endure the same death as my family.

"Elizabeth. She is behind all of this."

"Okay. So you kill Elizabeth. Will everything be as it was then?"

I look up at her, shaking my head. No. They will never come back. No matter how many rogues I take down, they will never come back.

"So you're sure you're mad at Elizabeth? Not anyone else?"

It's as if my breath is taken away from me as Lisa speaks, asking the question I am not prepared for. The question I know I have been avoiding.

"Me. I'm angry with myself. I never should have let Elizabeth go. I never should have let this happen. This is all on me!" I shout, slapping a hand to my chest.

Stubborn tears roll down my cheeks, which I furiously wipe away, my body shaking.

Lisa stares at me again.

Was this her point? For me to admit that yes, in fact, this was all my fault? That above all the rogues in the world, I loathe myself for poor judgment? That even through all of my father's training, I still failed this pack?

"You need to forgive yourself, Mae. In order to be at peace with their deaths and Lucas's state, you need to forgive yourself," Lisa says, placing a hand on my shoulder as she gives me a small smile.

I watch after her as she exits the kitchen and takes two steps at a time to the third floor. I know she is right. I have to come to terms with my own mistakes to let Mason and Natalie go. But how can I do that? How can I forgive myself for killing two people?

I sit on the kitchen stool, my hands placed in my lap as I watch my thumbs twiddle.

She makes it sound so easy. Just forgive. As if it is a simple phrase that will make all the problems disappear. However, nothing will change. I may accept that maybe I am not the sole reason that this happened, but that won't change the fact that they're dead, that half my pack is badly injured, and that Jesse can hardly look at me.

Then again, why should I forgive myself? Why should I dismiss the pain I caused and rid myself of the guilt and loss of those around me? I did do this. I should suffer the consequences and live every day knowing I killed Trent's and Jesse's mates. I shouldn't have the luxury of just wishing it all away as if it were nothing.

I think back to Lucas who has lived his whole life suffering the consequences of a mistake he made: jumping in front of his already dead father. His punishment was being mute. But now, he has come to terms with it. He came to terms with it when he exiled half of his pack. He came to terms with it when he spoke to me those two times. Even though his mistake only impacted himself, he still forgave and he lives with his disability, not as if it is a downfall but instead, a part of who he is. So if he can do it, why can't I?

Because you want everyone else to forgive you first.

But I shouldn't have to live off other people's opinions and their will to forgive. This is my life, my decisions. I have to forgive myself before others can as well.

Taking a deep breath, I close my eyes and let my shoulders sag forward. "You are forgiven."

Eighteen

Mae

October 20, 2036

 Since the time Lisa told me to forgive myself, everything has changed. I called my father and spoke to him. He admitted that when he was at his low, he did feel some sort of anger towards me, claiming it was my fault. However, he did apologize. I also spoke to Jesse; she still hasn't forgiven me, yet she no longer has distaste for me.
 The pack is healed. All the members who were injured have recovered with minimal damage. We have already begun training, strengthening. We will not let this happen again.

Lucas is still out. No movement, no noise, no sign of improvement. Travis looks at me with pity, and I know what he is thinking.

How long am I going to keep my mate like this?

Lucas spoke my name. I am not going to let him die knowing that he has something that needs to be said. I am not pulling the plug on this. He will stay in a coma until he wakes up, and he will wake up. He doesn't have a choice.

As of now, I am in my wolf form, lying on the cool forest floor, staring up at the trees as squirrels and birds flit from one branch to another. The sounds of nature surround me, bringing me such peace and tranquility. It's almost as if nothing can touch me while I am out here. The world and all of its problems are gone, just for these few moments.

I am, again, the mateless child who would go on runs for hours and lie on the forest ground to listen to nature. I am the girl whose biggest problem was deciding what to eat for lunch or dreading the next alpha lesson. I am the girl who only ever dreamed of finding a mate as perfect as Lucas.

Just for this moment, I am that girl again.

A twig snaps to my left, and I look over to see Travis in his wolf form, looking down at me as his tongue lolls out. He is panting as his mind races. He is anxious, in havoc. I jump to my feet, looking at him with concern.

What's happened? I ask, assuming the worst.

Another attack? Lucas passed in his sleep? Elizabeth is back?

He's awake, Travis says.

I stare at him for a brief second before my wolf shoots off and sprints towards the house as fast as my four legs can carry me.

He's awake...

I know he would wake.

Shifting and accepting a dress from a pack mate, I run into the house and up the stairs, taking two at a time until I am at our bedroom door. I throw it open, my eyes immediately going to the bed where Lucas is sitting up, leaning against the headboard.

"Oh my—" I don't finish as I fling myself onto the bed, gathering Lucas in my arms.

He lets out a sigh of content as he clings to me, his fingers digging into my back. He buries his face into my shoulder, placing open mouth kisses along my neck.

You're alive, he whispers.

I smile, nodding as I pull back to place my hands on both of his cheeks. "You're the one who gave me a fright. I thought I lost you, Luc."

Lucas brushes away the stray tear that escapes my eye, a small smile on his lips.

Never going to happen, little wolf.

His voice is like warm honey. I almost forgot what it sounded like. Almost.

"You don't know how happy I am right now." I rest my forehead against his, closing my eyes as I situate myself on his lap, arms looped loosely around his neck.

Lucas runs his fingers up and down my spine.

I have a good idea. He chuckles, giving my nose a soft kiss. *So, what did I miss?*

Sighing, I lean back against him and play with the hair at his nape. "In the end, we won. The rogues retreated. There were some casualties along the way. Natalie…and Mason. They—they didn't make it."

Lucas lets out a noise of discontent. He tucks a piece of hair behind my ear.

I am so sorry, mo ghrá. I know how close you were to them.

I shrug my shoulders, not wanting to get too deep into that conversation.

"Aside from that, the pack is nearly fully recovered. We're training, maintaining patrols, and ensuring the pack's safety."

Lucas holds a proud smile.

I am glad you didn't wait around for me, Mae. Though, I do recall hearing you say goodbye.

My eyes widen slightly. He heard me say that? He was conscious during my whole speech about how he deserved a better life, and how reluctant I was to actually say goodbye to him.

"I-I thought—you were unconscious—I thought you were dead." I stumble like an illiterate, slightly ashamed of myself for my lack of ability to speak while Lucas only finds it amusing. "It was the hardest thing I've ever done. So don't you ever put me in that position again." I growl, placing a finger to his chest.

Lucas laughs, nodding. *Fine by me.*

"As much as I want to be greedy and keep you all to myself, you need to see the pack," I say.

Lucas nods, letting out a quiet sigh before he slowly gets out of bed. He tests his legs for this is the first time he's been on them in a week. I watch the muscles in his back tighten as he tenses, waiting to fall flat on his face. However, his legs hold him up without much effort.

Lucas smiles to himself slightly and shuffles, testing the weight limit. He then glances over his shoulder at me, and I smile back before my eyes settle on the scars on his chest, his very naked chest…Taking a deep breath, I head to the closet to grab him a t-shirt.

They're not too bad, he says, his fingers running over the raised skin.

I flinch slightly, holding out his shirt as I desperately want him to cover up. Mostly because if he doesn't, I will keep him in this room until tomorrow evening and slightly because seeing the scars anger me. They nearly killed him.

Once Lucas is ready, he grabs my hand and leads me out of the bedroom, constantly squeezing my fingers as if to make sure I'm still with him. I stare at the back of his head, arching an eyebrow. He's needing contact more than I am, and I'm the one who have lived this last week without him.

I was conscious of everything that was happening. I knew when you were with me and when you weren't. It's safe to say I went a little mad lying completely still in silence, all alone.

I scrunch my eyebrows together, frowning. I can't even imagine the torture he had been through, knowing that I was there but he can't touch me.

"I'm sorry. I knew I should have stayed with you."

I'm glad you didn't. You would have regretted spending a whole week doing nothing.

I nod, not responding since we are now in the kitchen where Lisa encases Lucas in a tight hug. I drop his hand and stand back as Lucas reunites with his friends.

As he speaks with Travis and Jake, Lisa side steps over to me and whispers in my ear, "Did he speak again?"

I shake my head, crossing my arms as I watch the three men goofing off, throwing punches, and showing off their muscles.

I don't want to bring it up to Lucas that he spoke my name. I want him to find out on his own and speak only when he is ready.

"Not yet," I whisper back, letting out a sigh.

Lucas jerks his head to look at me, an eyebrow arching at the noise I made. I shake my head, offering a small smile. I don't want him to stop talking to Travis and Jake because if he does, I won't be able to stare at him as though I'm some creepy stalker.

All I want to do right now is just look at him, watch how he laughs, smiles, how the muscles in his arms flex when he reaches for a cup of orange juice, or watch his butt when he walks to the silverware drawer to grab a fork for pancakes. But of course, Lucas has other things in mind as he crosses our distance and places his hands on either side of my face.

Lucas leans down and presses the sweetest of kisses on my lips. My heart races, and in this moment, I forget about all the death and sadness that seems to be hovering over every Cipher pack member.

"Yeah, you guys are cute. We get it," Travis grumbles. "You need to address the pack."

All seriousness is brought back, and I softly glare at Travis. Can't we just spend a few moments as if everything hasn't changed?

Lucas places a kiss on my forehead and gives me a wink. *I love you.*

"Love you."

Lucas turns and heads outside to where the pack is already assembled. Lisa and I walk after him with Travis and Jake behind us.

The pack is overjoyed to see their alpha alive and healthy. Even when Lucas speaks about strengthening our defenses and how we have to be prepared for another attack, the pack is still in high spirits. Once Lucas is done speaking, they all gather around him, individually welcoming him back.

I am prideful at that moment. My alpha has a true family in his pack. Some alphas work extremely hard to gain the trust he seems to be given so easily, and to think that only a few months ago, half of his pack was aiming to kill him. This whole pack used to be in turmoil but not anymore. And whether he sees it or not, it's all because of him.

"Are you going to tell him?" Lisa asks.

I am confused for a moment, but I soon understand that she is referring back to our previous conversation.

"No. I think it's something he should do on his own. Think how happy and proud he will be if he discovers in his own time," I whisper to her.

Travis comes up beside me, bumping my shoulder with his.

"I wonder if it's completely back or if it's just what we've been practicing," Travis says.

I tilt my head slightly before I turn to face him. Travis's eyes widen slightly as if he were a kid caught with his hand in the cookie jar.

"Crap. I did not just say that."

"He's been learning how to say my name?"

"Mae, I didn't say that! Alright?" Travis is in a state of panic.

I've never seen him like this before. I would have stressed him further if it weren't for the fact that Lucas has been working with Travis, trying to say my name.

At this moment, I want to burst into tears of joy and tackle my mate to the ground. My heart can't be filled with anymore love than it has now. Lucas is so thoughtful, so selfless especially when it comes to matters concerning myself. How frustrating and difficult is it to modify the grunts and groans he makes into my name? Is it painful?

I want to ask him, but what if he doesn't want me to know? I don't want to ruin the moment he's probably been preparing for. Knowing Lucas, he has a date set in his mind when he wants to say my name. Not when he is nearly dying.

Should I just pretend I didn't hear it?

Pretend all you want.

I jerk my head up to look at Lucas with wide eyes. He smiles softly, reaching over to tuck a piece of hair behind my ear.

I remember speaking your name, Mae. And no, that wasn't when I wanted to do it, but it's done.

I let out a shaky breath as I stare into his eyes, a smile on my lips. "Can you—"

Lucas steps impossibly close, arms wrapping around my waist as he clings me tightly to his chest. His lips brush my ear as he whispers as soft as honey, "Mae."

Nineteen

Mae

October 20, 2036

"Lucas?"

"Hmm?" Lucas moans in response.

We are currently lying in bed with my head resting on his chest after making up for a week of lost time. It's around ten at night. I know Lucas isn't asleep. He told me a while ago that he doesn't fall asleep until he knows for a fact that I already am.

Isn't that just so darn cute?

Lucas's arm is wrapped around my back, his fingers lightly running up and down my arm. I draw lazy circles on his chest, playing with the thin blond hair that is barely visible.

"What's my name?" I whisper.

Lucas laughs, causing me to tilt my head back the same moment he shifts so when he bows his head, our foreheads are pressed together.

"Mae."

I will never get used to hearing Lucas say my name. Even though it's not his actual voice, it still gives me a peek of what it used to sound like. I am perfectly content with hearing his raspy, moaning voice.

I smile like an idiot, reaching up and running my fingers through his soft hair. "Again…" I beg.

"Mae."

I close my eyes and take a deep breath, pressing closer to him.

"Hmmm. I love you," I say, placing a kiss to his chin, just below his bottom lip.

Lucas quickly flips us over so he is hovering over me and I am lying underneath, my hand still buried deep in his hair. I smile, pulling him down close to me, his warm chest pressed tight against my breasts.

I love you so much more, mac tire beag (little wolf).

Lucas leans down, capturing my mouth with his in a searing hot kiss. I arch my back as he slide a hand between my spine and the bed. His fingers trace the length of my spine, causing chills to cover my body.

My legs wrap around his waist, pressing my body even closer to his as he trails kisses down my neck and along my collarbone. His tongue skims down to my breasts, where he leaves open kisses. I couldn't get enough of him.

Nearly losing Lucas puts everything in perspective. I will never take time with him for granted.

I heard you speaking about a son, Lucas says, pulling back to look down at me.

I'm panting as I look into his eyes. "Y-yes. I was regretting at that moment that you'd never be a father," I say, arching an eyebrow.

Lucas smile, nipping at my nose. *Then let's change that.*

My eyes widen as he captures my mouth again. I moan, clinging to him as he gently ensured that tonight is the night we will get pregnant.

* * *

When I wake up the next morning, Lucas isn't in the bed. I don't think too much about it. He probably wants to be as far from the bed as possible.

After taking a quick shower and pulling my hair up into a wet, messy bun, I dress in track shorts and a simple t-shirt. I don't bother with makeup. It's just a hassle, and there is no one I'm trying to impress. I already have Lucas, and there is no way he is getting away from me even if I do look like Godzilla.

I trot down the stairs, happiness overflowing inside me as I see Lisa sitting at the breakfast bar. She gives me a wave, smiling as I skip to her side.

"I guess being away from your mate for a week calls for endless, obnoxious, house-shaking love making," Lisa says.

My cheeks flame red as I giggle. I am not ashamed of what happened last night. Lucas wants a baby, and so do I, and there is only one way that is going to happen…

"Don't be jealous," I say, grabbing an apple from the bowl of fruit, biting into the sweet Honeycrisp. "Where are the men?" I ask.

"Alpha-beta meeting," she says with a casual shrug.

Without thinking about it, I turn and head towards the office where I push the big oak doors open.

"We have to go find her!" I hear Travis yell at Lucas.

Lucas doesn't get a chance to answer when they hear me come in. However, I didn't miss the murderous looks they both shared for each other. Lucas's expression quickly transforms as he casts me a breathtaking smile.

Good morning, baby, he says.

I take a hesitant step into the office, looking at Travis who is seething.

"Am I interrupting?" I ask, stepping beside Lucas.

He wraps an arm around my shoulder and gives the side of my forehead a kiss.

No. We were just finishing, Lucas says, but the look on Travis's face says otherwise.

He glares, crossing his arms.

"Alright. What is going on?" I ask.

"I was just telling Lucas how we need to find Elizabitch and figure out all there is to know about this rogue uprising," Travis tells me.

"So what's the problem? I think that's a brilliant idea."

"Well, Lucas doesn't." Travis growls.

I turn to look up at Lucas, pulling my eyebrows together.

"What? You just want to let her get away?"

Lucas lets out a sigh, shooting Travis a deadly look before he turns to face me. *We can't just go searching for her. What will happen when we find her? Torture her? She's an elder.*

"No. She was an elder. Now she's the woman who organized the retaliation that killed my aunt and uncle and nearly took you away from me!"

Lucas frowns, crossing his arms over his chest just like Travis. However, he's giving me the crossed arms.

Mae, I don't agree with unnecessary violence.

"Unnecessary?" Travis lets out a low whistle and claps his hands together. "Yes. I think you got it from here, Mae. Knock him dead," Travis says, giving my shoulder a squeeze as he retreats from the office.

Baby. I really don't want to argue about this with you. Lucas cups my face with his hands, his thumbs rubbing along my cheekbones.

I sigh, closing my eyes.

"Lucas, she broke me. I have to find her. Make her repay for what she did. What she did to you. Natalie...Mason." I choke when I get to Mason's name, tears welling in my eyes.

Lucas waits until they fall when he kisses them away. *Shhh. There has to be another way.*

I shake my head, stepping away from him. "Why are you so against finding her? We have to figure out what we're up against. We have to make her pay for all the lives the rogues took! Why don't you care?" I shout, shoving his chest when he tries to console me. "You didn't lose anyone during this fight, Luc! But I did! I lost two very important people, and I almost lost you! I need to make this right!"

Killing her is going to make this right?

"Her and every other rogue there is." I growl, hating how he is against this.

I have thought that out of everyone, he will be against the rogues. They slaughtered his family, most likely under Elizabeth's command, and he just wants to let her go?

Mae...This isn't you. You're not violent like this...You are a very reasonable alpha and you just need to take a deep breath.

"You sound like my father." I turn and run a hand through my hair, taking a deep breath.

But Lucas is right. My father taught me to always be calm, to never act so irrationally. Second chances are to be given. But wasn't she given one after she had the alpha family killed? He also taught me that it is never right to torture someone, to want to kill an innocent person.

She is not innocent.

"If you had died, Luc—"

"Mae..."

"If you had died, I honestly don't know what I would have done. I saw you, lying there, dead, and all I could think about was how there is no way I can live without you. So now you want her to recuperate, where she can bring back an army and who knows what will happen then. Maybe I will be saying goodbye to you for real, and I-I can't...I can't do that again!"

This time, I don't stop Lucas when he steps forward and wraps me up in his arms, tucking me under his chin. He rubs his hands up and down my back, gently soothing me.

Okay. Okay, baby. We'll do what you want. I just hate seeing you like this, Lucas says, pressing a kiss on the top of my head.

I squeeze onto him tightly, never wanting to let him go. Every moment we're apart, I think for a moment that he's dead, that somehow him coming back is all just a dream and the pain and heaviness in my heart is explainable.

"You can't leave me," I whisper.

I'm never going to.

Twenty

Mae

October 22, 2036

    Lucas kept true to his promise. He sent ten gammas out in search for Elizabeth. They are not to pursue her, only find her whereabouts and report back to us. We don't want the lives of the gammas to be at risk. If they storm one of the rogue campsites, they're as good as dead.

    I know Lucas opposes this idea. He is much like my father in this way. They both believe to live in peace, to not try and put a stop to a very serious threat but to sit back and wait for another attack, living in the moment.

    But I am at odds with them. After seeing members of my family killed, I refuse to let another opportunity arise.

Even if it does go against all the alpha lessons my father taught me. I won't let another loved one die.

Currently, I am sitting on the living room couch, flipping through a magazine that is sitting on the coffee table. However, I am not reading or paying attention to what is on the pages. My focus is on Lucas, who is sitting at the kitchen table behind me, eating his breakfast. He has been quiet these last two days, barely conversing with me.

I wonder if he is angry with me...

You've gone through that magazine three times already. Lucas's voice pops into my head, and I even jump a little, surprised.

I look over my shoulder to watch as a perfectly formed eyebrow rises as he nods to the magazine in my hands.

What are you thinking about? he asks.

After slapping the magazine close, I toss it on the table as I get to my feet and walk over to stand beside Lucas. He turns in his chair to gaze up at me.

"I'm thinking about that tattoo on your chest," I whisper, tucking my bottom lip between my teeth.

Lucas crosses his arms, sighing heavily.

Dearthàir. It means brother, Lucas says, scratching his arm absentmindedly.

I know talking about Gavin brings up bad memories. I find it humbling and very attractive that he has a tattoo in honor of his brother.

I give him a slanted smile, reaching over to touch his newly sprouted beard. He leans into my touch, his brown eyes remaining on me as he gives my palm a kiss.

"I've been wanting to ask since I first saw you shirtless in the forest, the day I found out you were my mate," I say, sitting down on the chair beside him.

Lucas finds my hand, tangling our fingers together.

"You were such a jerk," I mumble.

Lucas laughs wholeheartedly. Hearing it makes my stomach flutter with butterflies. He honestly doesn't know what he does to me.

I was trying to protect you…

"Yeah, yeah. You were stupid to think I'd ever let you just walk away." I roll my eyes dramatically, yet I am serious. I never would have let him leave without giving us a chance.

And now, I love you with all that I am. Go figure.

"Go figure…"

Lucas leans over, intent on giving me a long, passionate kiss, but it's cut into a short peck when the back door is opened. I look over my shoulder to see Jake running in, soaking wet.

Hmmm…When did it start raining?

Thunder and lightning crack, causing me to jump a little. I hate thunder…I hate the way it shakes the house and the ground. It feels as if the ground will just crack open and swallow me whole.

"Morning, Luna, Alpha." Jake nods to the both of us as he shuffles into the kitchen, leaving a muddy, wet trail behind him.

"Hey! Shoes off! And go take a shower!" I holler after him.

I really want today to be a low-key, lie on the sofa day with no rogues, Elizabeth, or dirty floors in mind. Now I have muddy footprints all over the beautiful wooden floors.

"Sorry, Luna Mae!" Jake yells from the kitchen.

I roll my eyes and cast a look over at Lucas. He stands, leaning down to place a kiss to my forehead.

I'll clean it up. Return to your fourth round of that magazine. Lucas smirks, ruffling my hair before he retreats into the kitchen to get cleaning supplies.

I have the best mate ever.

I gladly plop down on the couch, curling into a ball as I let the sound of rain lull me to sleep.

*   *   *

I wake up around two in the afternoon, with a blanket placed over me and my head on Lucas's lap. I peek up to see Lucas watching the silent TV, his face expressionless. He looks tired as well…

Why didn't he take a nice Wednesday afternoon nap with me?

Lucas is running his fingers through my hair, and I am convinced he has been doing so since I fell asleep at eleven. He is always too affectionate, always touching my hair or holding my hand, not that I am complaining. I absolutely adore the fact that he wants me within reach.

You were out like the dead, Lucas says, bowing his head to look down at me.

I stretch, letting out a moan for good measure as my bones crack. "Hmmm...That was much needed. Thank you."

Lucas smiles softly, continuing to massage my head as he returns his attention to the TV. I snuggle into him, craving the warmth only he can give me.

I can hear Travis sitting in one of the armchairs. He has remained silent, which is odd for him. He must be using a lot of willpower and restraint from talking Lucas's ear off.

"May I speak now?" Travis complains.

"No."

No.

Lucas and I say at the same time. I suppress my laughter as I hear Travis groan in distaste.

"He is in timeout?" I ask Lucas.

He's been very bad today. Forgot to run his patrol this morning.

I fake gasp, sitting up to look over at Travis with a hard glare.

"Travis! You know you can't forget your patrol!"

Travis has his arms crossed as he sulks in the chair, glaring at the empty fireplace.

"Yes. Yes. I know. Can I please go now? Jake wants to play Call of Duty."

I scrutinize him as if I am checking to see if he really did learn his lesson.

You're dismissed, Lucas grumbles, waving him off.

Travis jumps from the chair and bolts upstairs. I laugh as Lucas smiles up at me, shaking his head.

"Why exactly did he have to be silent?" I ask, pressing into his side.

Lucas drapes an arm around my shoulder. *I didn't want him to wake you up.*

His answer makes me feel like a princess. Lucas is too nice to me...Placing a blanket over me as I sleep, playing with my hair, and ensuring Travis doesn't yap me awake, I've truly been blessed.

* * *

It is a few days later that I find myself kneeling over the toilet bowl in our bathroom, experiencing the pleasures of morning sickness. Lucas is out with Travis, discussing Elizabeth's whereabouts.

The gammas found her. She's somewhere off in Kentucky. A far distance. Now that we know where she is located—we have a trained tail on her at all times—we have to come up with our next course of action.

I am totally prepared to fight this heathen and make her pay for what she did. However, now that I am carrying a child, I will not partake in this fight. I won't risk my baby's life, the way my mother did.

I can't wait to tell Lucas the news. He will be delighted, thrilled when he sees the small baby bump I now have.

Werewolves' pregnancies are the same length of that of wolves. Two and a half months. It's no surprise I'm already showing a little.

I decide to wait until Lucas gets back from his meeting. So I go lie on our bed, curled up in a ball as I wait for him to return. As I do so, I begin to think of names. If it's a boy, we should go with Mason or Gavin. A girl, Natalie or Shaye. Shaye is a beautiful Gaelic name which means admirable. I will be happy with any of those names. It's Lucas's job to narrow it down.

Lucas...Oh, I can't wait to see the look on his face when I tell him he is going to be a father. A wonderful one, at that. He has the natural instinct of caring for others and making people feel safe. The way he places a blanket over me or the way he plays with my hair...I know he will do well to make sure our baby is always safe and loved.

I hear the back door open and close, signaling that they are home.

Mae? Lucas calls for me.

Upstairs, I whisper.

I hear Lucas bound up the stairs, probably taking two steps at a time for he is at the door in a matter of seconds. When he steps into the room, he looks over at me with a concerned look on his face.

Are you alright? he asks.

I smile, nodding quickly as I sit up. "I have something to tell you."

Lucas lets out a deep breath and walks over to take a seat on the bed beside me.

What is it? Lucas grabs hold of my hand, tracing the lines on the inside of my palm as he stares into my eyes.

I bite my bottom lip as I can't help the excitement from growing.

"You're going to be a dad," I say, taking our joint hands and placing it on my slightly risen belly.

Lucas's face goes blank for a split second, processing what I am saying before he beams like a kid in the candy store.

Lucas drops to his knees, holding me tightly as he places his forehead against my stomach.

Páiste mo chroí, geallaim grá agus cherish agus tú a chosaint go léir na laethanta de do shaol. Is breá liom tú, mo hóga milis. (My dear child, I promise to love and cherish and protect you all the days of your life. I love you, my sweet pup.)

Twenty-One

Mae

December 5, 2036

    A lot has happened in the last month. Apart from my growing belly, we have pursued Elizabeth, effectively capturing her. A gamma, specially trained in receiving information from someone, has been torturing her in every way. However, she is loyal to her cause, never saying a peep.
    One day, I believe last Thursday, I went down to speak to her. I thought maybe having a one-on-one conversation with no torture would get her to spill, playing good cop, bad cop. But she only spat on my face and cursed the child in my womb. Then she cackled as if she were a witch and kept repeating "You're all dead."

Lucas was furious. *How dare she threaten our unborn child*, he said.

I was livid as well, but I never imagined he would run to the cells and wrap his hand around her throat. I had never seen that side of him, one that totally snapped and was full of rage.

It took me a good few minutes to calm him down.

Lucas contacted the packs, explaining what Elizabeth had said. My father agreed to send warriors to help with patrol. Our neighboring packs are also contributing.

Other than that, the last month has been uneventful.

I am now curled up in an armchair beside a cooking fire with hot cocoa in my hand and a blanket laid over my legs. This is one of the reasons I liked winter—snuggling in the warmth and drinking hot cocoa daily without being judged.

Lucas is out on a run, insisting that I stay indoors while he settles his wolf. I am aching for a run. I honestly hate sitting inside, not being able to breathe the fresh air, but I know it is dangerous for the baby if I shift.

I smile, placing a hand on my belly. We have decided to wait for the birth to find out the sex. We are aching for the surprise. Lucas agreed on the names Mason and Shaye. I was surprised he didn't want Gavin to be the baby's name. He simply told me that having someone to call Mason again would bring me absolute happiness. That was the end of the conversation.

As I've said many times, Lucas is selfless.

The baby kicks, causing me to gasp slightly.

What? I hear Lucas ask.

Not a moment later, the back door is thrown open as he is running in. Sweat is dripping off his forehead, his eyes wild, and hair plastered to his skin.

Men who run are so attractive. I remember back to when I thought that the first time Lucas and I went running together. And now here we are…I am carrying his child.

Lucas drops to his knees in front of me, grabbing hold of my hands.

"It's okay. It's okay. The baby just kicked. Here, feel." I grab his hand and place it on my belly.

I am now equivalent to a human being pregnant for six months. I watch as Lucas stares at my belly, his bottom lip caught between his teeth as he waits for the baby to kick again. When it does, Lucas lets out a throaty chuckle, and he reaches up to give me a hot kiss.

I love you so much, he says.

Even now, my heartbeat falters when he says that. I can never get enough of hearing those words.

"I love you too." I smile.

Lucas stands to his feet, taking the hot cocoa out of my hands as he uses his free hand to pull me to my feet.

Come. I'm taking you out, Lucas says.

"Oooh. Like a date?" I arch an eyebrow, grinning like an idiot.

Lucas scratches the back of his neck nervously. *Yeah. I've realized we have never been on a proper date…*

I reach up and run my hand through his hair. "You're so sweet. Alright, let's do this thing. But you need to help me get dressed."

Lucas already has me in his arms, carrying me as if I were a baby, up to our bedroom.

I instruct him, telling him I want to wear my favorite dress. However, it doesn't fit because of my large belly. I soon grow frustrated as all the nice clothes I have don't fit me anymore.

"Just go!" I yell at Lucas, throwing a wadded up red dress to the ground, storming into the closet as I try desperately to find something I can wear.

Mae...

"I don't even want to go on this stupid date, and now I have to find a dress that fits me, which none do because I'm a fugly planet!" I scream.

Of course, I want to go on this date. I want to go so badly, which is why I am so angry I can't find the perfect outfit. I hate myself for saying that to him.

You're beautiful, Mae, Lucas says.

"No, I'm not! Have you seen me? I waddle around like a penguin. I am throwing up nearly everything I eat. Oh, and I eat as if I was Travis on steroids! And now I have no clothes that fit me! Just, please go so I can figure this out!" I rip another dress off a hanger, looking at it as I hear Lucas leave the room.

I can't help but feel the pain he is experiencing right now. I have hurt him, and I mentally scold myself for doing so. Why am I so rude to him? Why am I so short-tempered with him all of a sudden?

After trying on every dress, I sit on the bed as I try to think of what to do. What am I going to wear if nothing fits? Lucas is so sweet to want to take me out, and I am completely ruining this for him. A tear rolls down my cheek, which I wipe away.

The bedroom door opens again, and I look up to see Lucas walk in holding a beautiful, floor-length purple dress with two-inch straps, an open back, and a slit that runs up the right leg.

It's one of my mother's maternity dresses, Lucas says, laying it on the bed beside me.

I look up into his eyes to see the sorrow in them—the sorrow that consumes his very being when I first met him, the sorrow I hope to never see again.

Mae, you are the most beautiful woman in this world. Carrying my child only makes you more so. I know it gets frustrating when nothing goes according to plan. Lucas kneels in front of me, placing his hands on my knees. *But, baby, I promise that it's alright. You don't have to wear the fanciest dress or anything other than sweats. Because I love you with all that I am, and not being able to fit into a dress is not going to change that. Now, if you want to wear my mother's dress, I am sure she will be honored that you did. If not, I am totally fine with you wearing sweatpants on our date.* Lucas leans forward and places a kiss to my cheek.

Letting out a soft sigh, I reach forward and wrap my arms around his neck.

"You're so wonderful to me," I say.

Lucas just holds me, running his hands up and down my bareback and over my bra. I bury my face into his neck, breathing in the scent of him. He smells of pine and fire. A hot, sexy combination.

"I would love to wear your mother's dress."

Lucas smiles, helping me to my feet as he gathers the dress and throws it over my head. The dress fits me like a glove, making me feel safe and comfortable. I look up at Lucas.

She labeled the month on the tag. She had every intention for her daughter-in-laws to wear some of her maternity clothes. I remember her telling Gavin how frustrating it is to find a dress that fits, and she didn't want our mates to go through it. Lucas explains to me, reading the obvious question on my face.

"She sounds like a wonderful mother," I say, placing a kiss to his cheek.

I wish I could have met her. I walk to the vanity mirror and brush my hair.

"Did Gavin have a mate?" I ask, looking at Lucas through the mirror.

His face falls slightly as he shakes his head.

No. Some girl out there is going to live her whole life mateless, Lucas says, walking up behind me. *I must confess something.* Lucas places a kiss to my right shoulder, his hands settling on my hips.

I tilt my head back as I continue to stare at us in the mirror.

"Alright."

I begged the Moon Goddess to take my life, that night of the Rogue Massacre. And when I was on my way of passing out, I thought I was actually going to die. The last thought on my mind was: my beautiful little mate is going to live the rest of her life in search for me, never fully satisfied or happy. I was extremely selfish, Mae. Because even as I thought that, I still wanted to die.

I turn in his arms to look up in his eyes.

And for that, I feel as if I owe you an apology. I'm sorry for ever having the thought of throwing what we have away.

I shake my head. "That's not selfish. That is a young boy not knowing how to live without his family. Lucas, you're the strongest, most selfless person I know." I reach up and place a kiss to his lips. "And I am glad you didn't die. You seem to have a knack for escaping death. There is nothing to forgive." I smile.

* * *

Lucas has made reservations for an extremely fancy Italian restaurant. He has been planning this for a long time. And to think I almost blow the whole date out of frustration and stupidity.

"I'm very sorry for blowing up at you today. I didn't mean anything I said. Well, other than the fact that I am a planet and I eat about as much as Travis in steroids."

Lucas smiles, reaching over to place his hand over mine.

The date has been going extremely smoothly. The waitress is gawking over Lucas, even asking about his scars and leaning on his chair. However, she grows disinterested when I explain that he can't speak due to an accident. Lucas finds it amusing, considering I am burning red with anger.

Does she not see this man impregnated me? Meaning we're the real deal...And that he is not in any way interested in some human girl?

The fork in my hand bends under pressure, causing Lucas to pry it from my grasp and try his best to reform it.

Mae...

I look up from my nearly empty plate, a small smile on my lips. Lucas looks nervous. Extremely nervous.

There is something I have to tell you...

"Alright. Whatever it is, we'll work it out together," I say, giving his hand a squeeze.

Lucas lets out a deep breath. "I don't know how, but I got my voice back the night I nearly died."

The deformed fork falls from my hand, clattering on the plate. I stare at Lucas with wide eyes as his voice overwhelms me. Just as I imagined. Deep, husky, with the smoothness of honey.

"W-w-wha-what?" I stumble, shaking my head. This has to be a dream. "W-why di-didn't you s-say something?"

"Because I was waiting for tonight. I was waiting until the exact moment where I take both of your hands in mine." As Lucas speaks, he does exactly as he says, "I look straight into your eyes and say, 'Mae Matthews, before you, I was a lost soul. I was surrounded by chaos and disorder. All I wanted was for my life to come to an end. But when I found you, you brought this light into my world. You are so full of happiness. You see the best in every situation. You try to make everything right. You are the most beautiful woman I have ever laid my eyes on. You have stolen my heart, my breath, my soul...I can't live in a world without you. Will you do me the honors of being my—'" Lucas is cut off by gunshots.

I freeze, jerking my head towards the restaurant entrance to see three men storming in with guns.

"Everyone out!"

My wolf shakes, nipping at the alpha voice that overcomes us. I know that voice.

I struggle to find the owner as all the humans flee the scene, leaving Lucas and I alone. I get to my feet, Lucas stepping in front of me as my eyes narrow on Duke. He walks fluidly over to stand in front of us, a smirk playing on his lips.

"Mae."

"Duke? What are you doing?" I ask in disbelief.

Duke raises the gun and points it to my head, causing me to tighten with fear. Lucas snarls, shoving me back a step and taking my place. The moment he does so, he is tackled to the ground by another alpha and a beta. Lucas struggles as the two wolves beat the daylights out of him.

"Stop it!" I growl.

After many punches, Lucas lies on the ground, groaning as he spits up blood. The second alpha grabs him by the back of the neck, his elongated claws piercing the skin as blood trickles down. He pulls Lucas up, having him kneel before me. The beta stands close as Duke steps forward, placing the pistol to my forehead.

"Why are you doing this?" My voice is shaking.

"Why? Why! I loved you, Mae! And you just left! Without a second thought, you left me! I thought what we had was special. All the flirting and the hugs...I thought we were getting somewhere until you left me." Duke snarls, his face red with anger as tears well in his eyes.

"Duke...you're my cousin. I could never love you like that..."

"We're not even related, Mae. I know you felt what I felt."

I shake my head.

"After you were gone, Lucas soon exiled the rogues. I knew how hostile they were towards their former alpha. So I asked Alpha Marcus' son, Kyle, to join my crusade. The beta is Oliver. He's my second. They were eager to help me win back my rightful mate. We approached the rogues, telling them our idea to bring down the Cipher pack, killing all but you. Soon, many more rogues joined in, and we had an army. But you are too intelligent, little mate. You were already producing an army on your own, seeing into Elizabeth's facade."

I cringe when he calls me his mate. It makes me feel agitated, and I'm repulsed. How can he even think I am his? I never was.

Duke walks forward and runs a hand over my cheek. "That's what I love about you, Mae. You're such a wonderful alpha," he whispers, placing a kiss to my temple.

"Get away from her!" Lucas snarls, getting to his feet only for Oliver to deliver a hard kick to his crotch. Lucas lets out a choking groan, falling to his side as I gasp.

"Don't hurt him!" I yell.

"Then you will come with me. You will become my luna. We will abort that abomination in your belly and have many children of our own," Duke says, a genuine smile on his lips.

That's what makes this sick. He actually believes everything he is saying.

"I'll never go with you. I will never kill my child." I snarl.

Duke doesn't blink as he lifts his gun and shoots Lucas in his right leg.

My mate lets out a deafening roar, causing me to shake in anger and pain.

"Luc!" I scream, dropping to my knees to grab his face in my hands.

He's all sweaty, his wolf desperately trying to heal his leg.

"It's going to be okay, baby..." I say, instantly earning a slap from Duke. The impact has me spiraling to the floor.

"That man is nothing to you! If you want him to live, you will come with me."

I shake my head, looking over at Lucas.

It comes down to this—Lucas's life or my child's. If I go with Duke, he will kill my baby, but Lucas will live. If I stay...he may still kill Lucas and then my child. Why will Duke do this to me? I thought we were friends.

"Lucas..."

"It's okay. Our child must live..." Lucas says, his eyes meeting mine.

I shake my head quickly.

"Mae..." *Kick in his knees.*

I look up to see Duke looking down at us, waiting. I take a few deep breaths as if I was contemplating my decision.

"Come o—" Duke didn't finish for I recoil my legs and kick outward, hitting his knees dead on. They bend inward, snapping under pressure.

Duke lets out a cry in pain as he falls forward. Oliver quickly advances to me. I hop to my feet and meet him halfway. He swings a fist my way, but I easily duck and snatch a steak knife off a nearby table. When he turns to advance me, I take a half step forward and shove the knife up under his ribcage, puncturing a lung.

I look over to see Lucas struggling with Kyle. His weight is kept off his injured leg as they fight. As I go to aid Lucas, another gunshot is fired. I feel the impact more so than the pain.

I am knocked to the ground, landing on my hands and knees as I look over to see a bullet hole just under my collarbone, near my right shoulder. Blood pours endlessly as I hear Lucas let out a growl. The world grows fuzzy and out of focus as I desperately try to hang on.

World swaying, I fall to my side. Tears roll down my cheeks as I think of the child inside of me. She is going to die because I am too weak. I am too weak to protect her.

I am sorry, mo hóga beag (my little pup).

Perhaps it is history repeating itself; my child dying just as my mother's did.

Twenty Two

Lucas

December 5, 2036

"We're losing her!" Stephen, the pack doctor, hollers as he wheels Mae into the infirmary.

I run beside the gurney, ignoring the pain in my leg as I grip tightly to her hand.

How can this happen? An evening meant to be filled with happiness and love suddenly turned to blood and tears. I am losing my Mae. After finally speaking to her, finally proposing, I wasn't strong enough to keep her alive. Or my child.

"You do everything you can to save her." I snarl at Stephen as we enter the emergency room.

All the nurses rally around him, instantly gearing up to help save their luna. I stand back, watching as they begin operating on her.

They remove the bullet from her shoulder easily, but she still doesn't heal. Why isn't her wolf healing her? The deafening sound of the flatline rings through the room as Stephen looks up at me.

"We can still save the child."

Tears roll down my cheeks as I step back, shaking my head.

"Lucas! You must decide! Operating on Mae could kill the child. If I deliver the child, we will be able to revive Mae."

I grip my hair, feeling my lungs constrict at what he says.

How?

She was just with me. I was holding her hand, staring into her beautiful hazel eyes. How can she be dead? How can I make the choice between child and mate?

My other half. My sole purpose for why I am still alive today. How can I live without her? But then our child. I can't kill it any more than I can kill Mae. They are both a part of me. Both the two lights of my life.

"Lucas!" Stephen yells.

I look up and shake my head.

"If you don't decide, we will save the baby."

I don't try to rein in the sob that shakes through me as he says this.

"Marie, prepare for the C-section."

I fall to my knees, unable to stand.

Why isn't Mae healing? That bullet shouldn't have killed her. So why did it?

I look up at the operating table. "Please save her," I whisper.

Stephen looks down at me, a frown on his face.

"Save them both."

*   *   *

Travis walks over and sits beside me as the operation continues to take place. They are trying to revive Mae, have been for the past hour. They were able to save the baby; however, I am unable to see her. She is premature, extremely weak and fragile. They are giving her intensive care to ensure she will survive.

I was kicked out of the operating room, and I am growing frustrated that Mae isn't waking up. Now I am sitting outside the door.

"It was a wolfsbane bullet that hit her."

I look over at Travis.

"But I have already healed."

"There were two guns at the scene. One had bullets laced with wolfsbane. Duke meant to kill her," Travis says.

I cringe at his words, clenching my hands into fists. I don't want to talk about her death because she is going to survive this. She has to.

"It's over, Luc. Duke is dead. The rogues are no longer going to harm us."

I look over at Travis.

"If Mae doesn't survive, I will hunt down every rogue and slaughter them. Then I will go to Duke's family and do the same. Because I will live every day in pain if she doesn't make it out of this."

Travis doesn't respond, only sits back in the chair and crosses his arms.

After another good thirty minutes, the doors finally open. I look up to see Stephen walk out, blood covering his gloves and shirt.

"She's stable. We had to go in and pump her heart manually after we rid her body of the wolfsbane. She should be fine, Alpha."

I let out a sigh, pushing away from my chair and rushing in to see Mae lying on a hospital bed now instead of an operating table. Her body is hooked up to machines, a breathing tube in her nose, a feeding tube down her throat, and IVs up to her arms. I don't care though. She's alive.

I grab a stool and place it beside her bed, grabbing her delicate hand in my own.

"I now understand the pain you went through, *mo cheann donn*. We are even now…" I lean forward and lay my head on her lap, burying my face into the blanket covering her as I allow myself to cry.

Nearly losing Mae was as if someone was taking away my means to live. I didn't know how to breathe, how to think…Losing her would have torn me apart, and I will thank the Moon Goddess every day that she didn't take her away from me.

I fall asleep with her hand in my own and my head on her lap, needing to feel her close to me.

I am awakened by a hand combing through my hair. Lifting my head, I see Mae looking down at me with tear-filled eyes. Jumping to my feet, I can't help but cover her face with kisses.

"Mae...Oh my sweet Mae," I whisper, burying my face into the crook over her neck.

Mae struggles to wrap her arms around me, weak and caught up in IV tubes.

When I pull back, tears roll down her cheeks. I feebly brush them away with my thumbs.

Our baby...I killed our baby, didn't I? Mae asks, unable to speak because of the breathing tube. Her voice is so broken, so shattered.

"No. No, baby. She's alive. Shaye is alive." I smile, resting my forehead against hers.

Mae lets out a sob as she clings to me.

I thought I killed her. I thought I killed her.

I shush her, rubbing her arms up and down as I try to comfort her.

Can I see her? she asks, looking around the room for a crib that Shaye should be sleeping in.

"She was premature. She's in intensive care. We won't be able to see her until she is a little stronger, little wolf," I say, sitting back down on the stool.

Mae lets out a sigh as she locks her eyes with mine.

What happened to Duke?

"Travis and Jake arrived just after you passed out. They handled Kyle while I finished off Duke. Everything is over, Mae. We no longer have to worry about attacks." I smile, trying to reassure her.

Mae nods, closing her eyes for a moment.

"I'm going to get Dr. Stephen." I place a kiss to her forehead before I go find the doctor to thank him for saving my mate and my child.

* * *

Mae was able to leave the infirmary the next day. We were also able to see Shaye; however, we cannot hold her. They keep her in an incubator to maintain her body temperature and no bacteria can get to her. Her wolf is helping in healing her rather quickly though. She is already growing, however, not enough for it to be safe to take her home.

I hold Mae in my arms as we lie on the couch in the living room, watching the fire as it crackles on the firewood. Lisa is making hot cocoa for Mae. Travis is flipping through channels, struggling to find a good show to watch. Jake is reading some mystery novel.

All of us sitting around each other feels good. It feels as if we are a family again with no fear of the rogues looming over us. If only Shaye is with us, then it would have been a perfect moment. Soon, though. Soon she'll be in our arms, and we will cherish and spoil her. She will always be in my arms, or Mae's, or Lisa's…and undoubtedly Travis's. He doesn't want to admit it, but he already loves his niece.

Lisa hands Mae her hot cocoa and sits beside Travis. Mae sips her drink, snuggling into me. Her injuries are fully healed now, and there is only a faint scar on her shoulder.

We all sit in silence until the back door is opened, and I look to see Dr. Stephen walk in. I instantly tense, causing Mae to jump to her feet and look at Stephen with wide eyes.

"I need to speak to you…"

Dr. Stephen takes us to the infirmary again, where we stand beside Shaye's incubator. We watch as he reaches a hand in, placing it beside Shaye's head where he snaps his fingers. I know something is supposed to happen—a tilt of the head, a wiggle of the body, or maybe even a cry—but there is no response.

Mae begins to cry, instantly blaming herself. "She wouldn't be deaf if she wasn't premature. She wouldn't be premature if I was able to protect her!" she yells at me.

I want so badly to comfort her, but I know nothing I say would take the guilt away from her. So, despite her struggles, I hold Mae beside our daughter who stares up at the ceiling with such wonder. So innocent…Our sweet Shaye will live her life with the struggle Landon Matthews and I both faced.

I can only hope she has a mate such as I had to help her get through the trials of her life ahead.

Epilogue

Lucas

February 2, 2054

    I stand beside Shaye as she clutches her arms to her chest, her body leaning forward, head bowed as sobs shake through her. Mason, my sixteen-year-old son, grabs one of her hands, giving it a tight squeeze as tears roll down his cheeks as well.

    As I stare at my two children, I can't help but think how perfect they are. Shaye has grown into such a beautiful young lady. She shares her mom's dark hair and hazel eyes. She is petite, just like her mother was. Mason has my blond hair, but he also inherited his mother's eyes. He is the same height as me and will most likely surpass me in the near future.

The two siblings are extremely close. As close as Gavin and I were…They feel each other's pain and protect each other from whatever danger presents itself.

Mason is strong. He is a powerful warrior. He has proven that on the battlefield.

I was wrong when I looked at my beautiful mate and told her that the danger was over, that the rogues would never harm us again. It just goes to show just how I fail at protecting my family.

I was looking into Jenny's eyes the moment she kicked Mae's knees in. Tyler had me in a headlock, forcing me to watch as my mate kneels in front of her aunt. Her aunt! They blamed us for Duke's death. I should have known this wasn't over…

Mae was crying as she shakes her head, screaming at me—"It's okay! Luc, it's okay!"—over and over until Jenny forever silenced her, slicing my mate's neck.

The pain was unbearable. I felt it. Mason felt it…Shaye felt it. The whole pack felt the death of their luna so instantaneously, and I just stood there, my body frozen as my mate was taken from me the same way my mother, father, and brother were so many years ago.

I remember letting out a loud roar that shook through the forest. However; I do not remember killing Jenny and Tyler in return. But it was quick, and I was soon holding Mae in my arms. I was shaking, feeling my soul, my will caving in on me. How can this happen? Why do the people I love always end up dying? Too soon…

Mae was thirty-six when she died. Too young. Too young for my beautiful mate. She had so much left to do.

So much left to see. I promised her we'd travel around the world, once the Cipher pack is passed down. But again, I was unable to keep my promise.

"Daddy…"

I snap out of my daze to look down at Shaye. Her cheeks are red, her eyes puffy as she nods to the casket in front of us.

Tears roll down my cheeks as I step forward and place a rose on the Oak casket…I remember Mae telling me just how much she loved the look of Oak when Travis and Jake broke our Oak table set.

"I am so sorry, my sweet Mae. I have failed you…I have failed to protect you…You deserved so much better. But I promise, I will not let this happen to Shaye or Mason. I will protect them until the day I die. I will not fail you again." I place a hand on the casket for a moment, letting out a deep, shaky breath.

I turn and walk over to embrace Shaye and Mason in a hug. I feel Shaye sob into my shoulder, and I just cling onto them.

My sweet Mae…It was never a child's dream to have a family. We created the best family, mo cheann donn. And I swear to the Moon Goddess that I will protect our family. But until I see you again, I will have to find you in Shaye's smile and in Mason's stubborn nature. I will find you in all that you have done with the strong, growing pack—the pack you saved and impacted. Until I see you again, I will continue to love you every day here on Earth until I can have you in my embrace again. Until I see you again, my sweet Mae.

THE END

Can't get enough of Mae and Lucas? Make sure you sign up for the author's blog to find out more about them!

Get these two bonus chapters and more freebies when you sign up at charlotte-michelle.awesomeauthors.org

Here is a sample from another story you may enjoy:

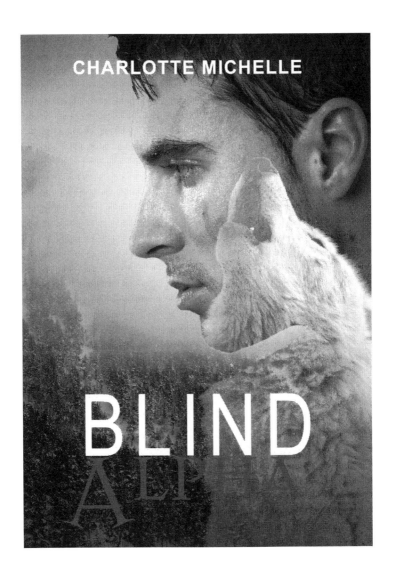

Prologue

Landon

March 8, 2010

"Father, be rational. We don't have a chance against the Prowler Pack. We're going to be annihilated." I place my hands on my father's desk, pleading for him to see reason.

His head is ducked down, avoiding eye contact, and ignoring me as he writes down war tactics. His salt and pepper hair is mussed and frantic, a sign that he hasn't showered, let alone comb his hair in what could be days. He now has a scruffy beard resting on his face. He clenches his fists, grinding his teeth as he tries to concentrate.

Caleb Matthews is a powerful Alpha. He is wise and patient. He doesn't think irrationally or acts upon impulses. He has been a role model towards me, and I am grateful to have him as a father. That is until my mother, his mate, was taken from us and slaughtered. Now, all that is on his mind is revenge, and it is clouding his reason. He is arranging a battle that we will not win. The Shadow Pack will die off tonight if he follows through with this.

Natalie, my little sister, is only seven years old. She has her whole life ahead of her. She is yet to see the beauty of finding her mate. She still has all her homecoming dances and prom. This wasn't how her life is supposed to unfold. She is far too innocent and kind to meet such a tragic end.

"Inform Cole that we strike in an hour." His voice is coarse, dry from the lack of nourishment. Having a weak Alpha only lessens our odds of winning.

"Father, please," I beg, dipping my head down so he can look into my eyes and see the reason I hold for the both of us.

"Now, Landon!" he snarls, head snapping up to give me a cold glare.

I square my shoulders and straighten my spine. I nod my head and turn to walk out of his office. Once the door is closed, I sprint up into Natalie's room.

I open the door to find her sitting on her bed, applying nail polish to her toes. Her head rises slowly, and tears instantly begin to gather. "No." She shakes her head.

I grab her from under the arm and lift her to her feet. "You are to leave with Tasha and her daughter. You will hide out in the cabin. You will not leave the cabin until I come get you, understood?"

Tears roll down her rosy cheeks as she nods her head. "What if you don't come back?" she whimpers.

"Then you are going to live a very happy life with Tasha and Sarah." I don't wait for Natalie to protest or ask another question. I squat to place a soft kiss on her forehead and give her a tight hug. I then stand to my feet and allow Tasha, Cole's Mate, to gather Natalie in her arms and exit the room in haste. I follow Natalie with my eyes until she is out of sight.

She deserves a long, happy life.

Cole, we strike in fifty, I tell my father's Beta. He doesn't respond, but I can feel his anger.

I exit the Pack House to see my best friend, Mason. He would have been my Beta if things were different. In two years' time, I'd be given the Alpha position, and he would be my right-hand man. Now, our futures and our lives end tonight.

Mason gives me a pat on the shoulder and offers me a smile. "We always said we'd go down swinging."

"Yeah, but I imagined us older, with mates and children to carry on our legacy. Not like this. Not so blindly and irrationally." I cross my arms, waiting for my father to finish in his office, waiting for my doom. Everyone's doom… besides Mason's. "Can you do something for me?"

Mason arches his right brow in question. "Anything."

"When it starts to turn ugly… when the Shadow Pack starts to go down, I want you to go to the cabin. Natalie, your sister, and your mother will be there. I want you to take them far away. Make sure Natalie lives a long and happy life."

"Landon—"

"Mason, I am asking you this not as your Alpha but as your friend. At least, one of us deserves to live through this."

Caleb Matthews decides then to join his pack. He steps onto the yard, and all the warriors shift into their wolves. I give Mason a look, and with a nod, I happily shift into my wolf.

No more words were said. There was nothing to say. It would all just fade in time, and no one would be alive to remember. With Caleb's transition into his wolf, we take off to the Prowler Pack.

The Prowler Pack is located a few miles north of the Shadow pack. We reach the territory within ten minutes. I come to position at the left of my father as Cole is at his right. Mason comes up on the other side of me, and I give him one last look. He nods at me one more time before my father lowers and wiggles his shoulders as if to pounce on a stag.

With a low growl, he charges forward to take down a Prowler on patrol. With that one kill, the whole pack has been alerted that we arrived. Another poor mistake made by my father. I shake my head. No going back now.

Prowler wolves soon outnumber us, and as we do well to fight them off, they soon overpower us. I watch as the Shadow's number dwindle. *Now, Mason!*

My friend shoves off a wolf and takes off towards my sister. I let out a growl as the wolf he was fighting follows him along with two others. He won't be able to fight them off. I cast one last look at my father and shoot a message to Cole. *Grab as many men as you can. Retreat.*

Even though I wasn't Cole's Alpha, he obeys my command. My father is lost, both figuratively and literally.

I chase after the three wolves following Mason. I can't allow them to get to my sister. No matter what, she will live.

I tackle a gray wolf to the ground, and we tumble, rolling. Twigs and rocks scrape at my sides, causing nothing but an annoyance. I snarl at the Prowler wolf, advancing on him. I pin him easily, chewing into his neck as I hear Mason say, I'm here. I managed to kill the wolf following me. Natalie is safe.

I was too consumed with joy at the news to put together what my Beta said. I should have been able to see the remaining wolf blindside me. I should have been able to counter his attack. Instead, I am the one who is pinned with a fatal slash across my face.

It seems my father wasn't the only one to make costly mistakes.

Chapter 1

Lana

February 15, 2014

February 15. It's my birthday. I'm finally eighteen, and all I can think about is how I am finally able to leave this awful pack. At the age of eighteen, female wolves are able to sense their mates, and I intend to find mine. And when I do, Alpha Castor Vang will have no claim on me. He will no longer be able to touch or hit me. I will be free, and I will be safe.

I pack my bags. Everyone is asleep. Castor is too wrapped up in the she-wolf in his bed to be paying attention to the stirring on the first floor. My father is a deep sleeper. He wouldn't even wake during an earthquake. I will not miss him or my mother. They don't deserve a second thought. They have allowed Alpha Castor to beat me. That's the price of being an Omega, I guess.

I grab an apple from the kitchen table and put it in my bag before I exit the house in haste. I get to the edge of the Cossitt Pack territory where my brother pulls me into a hug.

"Be careful," he whispers. Trent volunteered to take up patrol tonight so I could flee. He had always looked out for me, and this has been a day we've been looking forward to for a long time. "Never come back."

Even after years of begging, Trent still refuses to join me. He felt it was his duty to protect all the other victims of Castor's rage. After losing his wife and daughter, Alpha Castor turned brutal and abusive. Trent has always been the hero.

With my bag over my shoulder, I morph into my muddy brown wolf. I am not the most beautiful wolf, that much is certain. Being an Omega, my wolf is small, and my fur coat is a less than admirable color. However, being small does grant me the skill of being sly and quick.

I run from my old home without a glance back. I run until I no longer can.

Days pass, all I do is run. I occasionally stop to catch food or take a quick rest. But my breaks never last more than twenty minutes. If I don't keep running, I risk Castor catching up with me, and I can't allow that to happen.

It is only when starvation and exhaustion get the best of me that I make the mistake of stepping onto the Shadow Pack's land. I know of this pack. Their story is sad, gut-wrenching.

Alpha Caleb Matthews lost his mate, and in a blind rage, he took his pack to their death. He lost most of his warriors. If it weren't for his Beta, there wouldn't be a Shadow Pack anymore. Cole took a group of warriors and fled the fight. They returned to the women and children and were able to replenish the Shadow Pack.

That isn't the sad part, however. Alpha Landon Matthews, Caleb's son, was brutally wounded. He left the fight with his life but not his sight. His loss turned him cold, vicious. He didn't care for anyone.

That's why I knew I was royally screwed when two wolves stepped into my path. They look at me with mournful expressions. They know my fate as do I.

They shift to their human forms, and I bow my head to avoid eye contact with their nudity. I then hide behind a tree to shift and reach into my bag to pull on a simple sundress. I look at my muddy feet, frowning as I try to tame my wild hair.

I, at least, deserve to die looking my best.

"Come." I hear a low voice. I walk over to see two men, one with shaggy blond hair and the other with buzzed brown hair. They are both dressed in black track pants, leaving their chest exposed to the warm sun. There is no mistaking their strength. They can easily snap me in half.

They take position at my sides, walking me to the pack house. My stomach churns with my pending doom. I am going to die. I left one awful situation to enter another.

The pack house is fairly larger than the Cossitt Pack's. I can sense the distress that takes place on this property. They still haven't recovered from the massacre.

It's been four years. I guess no one would be able to recover from the loss of a loved one.

Blondie opens the door for me, and I step into the back entrance of the house. I take in the newly installed kitchen, the nicely furnished living room, and the grand staircase that leads upstairs. Shoulders nudge me, and I continue onward until we are in front of oak French doors.

Blondie knocks. "Landon, we found a trespasser."

I grimace at the name. Yes, I did trespass, technically. But I was running for my life… Doesn't that count for anything?

"Enter."

The buzzed boy grabs the doors and pulls them open, nodding for me to go in.

"I got it from here, Zane," Blondie says, grabbing my bicep roughly. I hiss at the pain, glaring at him. Zane leaves while I am dragged into the office.

The office is large with wooden floors and two rustic orange walls. One wall has floor-to-ceiling windows while the other has a built-in bookshelf. The office has a tray ceiling with an elegant five-arm chandelier that has a bronze finish. There is a rolled arm bench with a warm brown wood finish and is topped with a comfortable cream cushion that is placed in front of one set of the windows. There is a large, orange and red Persian rug underneath his wooden desk with two chairs that match the bench in front of it. And then, there is the man in the large brown leather chair.

I see Alpha Landon sitting at his desk, his head bowed down as he rests it in his hands.

"You know the protocol. Kill the rogue." Landon's voice is monotone, uncaring. He is willing to murder me off so easily. He doesn't even know who I am or what I've been through! "Why trouble me with this, Mason?"

"I'm not one to kill an innocent girl, Landon."

The Alpha lifts his head, almost as if he was trying to get a look at me. And when he does, I gasp.

Not because of the scars that adorn his beautiful face or the way that his eyes are fogged. I don't gasp because I am horrified of this man in front of me. I gasp because as I look into his hazy eyes, I know only one thing. He is my mate. I have found him, and I can't explain how incredibly happy it makes me feel. I have accomplished what it was I sought out to do.

Landon growls and snatches up his black Aviator sunglasses, covering his eyes.

"No!" I don't stop from crying out. I don't want him to hide from me, not ever. He's beautiful.

Landon holds the features of a pure god. His skin is perfectly sun-kissed to create a bronze tan. His shoulders are broad with strength and power. His jaw line is sharp, yet his cheeks are smooth. His brown wavy locks rest carefully on his head, a simple curl falling onto his forehead. I want nothing more than to run my fingers through his hair. I can tell through the haze of his eyes that they used to be a soft blue.

Mason tightens his grip on me, and I let out a cry.

"Ow!" I glare at him, waiting for Landon to lash out at Mason for laying a hand on his mate. That never happens, however. I look at Landon to see him glaring in my direction. "You're going to let him hurt me?" I am completely shocked. After all, I've heard mates are very protective and would never let any harm come to them.

"Why should I care if he hurts you?" he snarls, getting to his feet.

My wolf purrs with delight as I take in his sculpted body. The t-shirt he wears does a fabulous job at showing off his slim torso and every indent of his abs.

I gasp at what he says. Why should he care? Does that mean… "You reject me?" I see Landon's shoulders go rigid.

"Reject you?"

"Reject our mating. I've heard it happen before but—"

"Enough! I don't know who you think you are, but you are not my mate. I would know if you were! Since Mason has a soft spot for women, I will give you the rank of Omega, and you will work with the pack. Stay out of my way, and there will be no trouble. Got it?" he snaps. My eyes widen at what he says.

How can he not feel what I feel? It is so strong, so powerful. I know he's my mate. There is no mistaking it. I'd give my life for this man. So why doesn't he see me as I see him?

See… See. He can't see me! He can't see me, he can't look into my soul. Our souls can't connect. No. That's not possible. How am I to prove to him that I am his mate?

Would a simple touch prove to him? Or would it have to be something more personal than that?

Tears roll down my cheeks as Mason takes me away from my newly found mate.

No matter what it takes, I will prove to him that what I say is true. I will take away his pain and show him what it is to love again. I promise you this, my mate.

If you enjoyed this sample then look for **Blind Alpha.**

Other books you might enjoy:

His to Claim
Ashley Michelle
Available on Amazon!

Other books you might enjoy:

I'm the Alpha's Mate
Sydney Marie
Available on Amazon!

Introducing the Characters Magazine App

Download the app to get the free issues of interviews from famous fiction characters and find your next favorite book!

iTunes: bit.ly/CharactersApple
Google Play: bit.ly/CharactersAndroid

Author's Note

Hey there!

Thank you so much for reading The Mute Alpha! I can't express how grateful I am for reading something that was once just a thought inside my head.

I'd love to hear from you! Please feel free to email me at charlotte_michelle@awesomeauthors.org and sign up at charlotte-michelle.awesomeauthors.org for freebies!

One last thing: I'd love to hear your thoughts on the book. Please leave a review on Amazon or Goodreads because I just love reading your comments and getting to know YOU!

Whether that review is good or bad, I'd still love to hear it!

Can't wait to hear from you!

Charlotte Michelle

About the Author

I live in Oswego, Illinois. I am a shift manager at Starbucks and I am using the Starbucks Achievement Plan through Arizona State University to get my bachelors in English. My favorite spot to write is in my living room, sitting on the couch with my dog by my feet. My passion for writing is inspired by my grandfather, who is a professor at Harper College and holds a talent for writing himself.

Made in the USA
Columbia, SC
12 April 2019